I0609646

Metta Victoria Fuller Victor

A Bad Boy's Diary

Metta Victoria Fuller Victor

A Bad Boy's Diary

ISBN/EAN: 9783337196967

Printed in Europe, USA, Canada, Australia, Japan

Cover: Foto ©Andreas Hilbeck / pixelio.de

More available books at **www.hansebooks.com**

Frederick Warne and Co., Publishers,

NOTABLE NOVELS.

COMPLETE EDITIONS.

Large crown 8vo, SIXPENCE each, Picture Wrappers.

1	SCOTTISH CHIEFS.	Miss Jane Porter.
2	UNCLE TOM'S CABIN.	Harriet Beecher Stowe.
3	ST. CLAIR OF THE ISLES.	Elizabeth Helme.
4	CHILDREN OF THE ABBEY.	E. M. Roche.
5	THE LAMPLIGHTER.	Miss Cummins.
6	MABEL VAUGHAN.	Miss Cummins.
7	THADDEUS OF WARSAW.	Miss Porter.
8	THE HOWARDS OF GLEN LUNA.	Miss Warner.
9	THE OLD ENGLISH BARON, &c. &c.	Clara Reeve.
10	THE HUNGARIAN BROTHERS.	Miss Porter.
11	MARRIAGE.	Miss Ferrier.
12	INHERITANCE.	Miss Ferrier.
13	DESTINY.	Miss Ferrier.
14	THE KING'S OWN.	Captain Marryat.
15	THE NAVAL OFFICER.	Captain Marryat.
16	NEWTON FORSTER.	Captain Marryat.
17	RICHELIEU.	G. P. R. James.
18	DARNLEY.	G. P. R. James.
19	PHILIP AUGUSTUS.	G. P. R. James.
20	TOM CRINGLE'S LOG.	Michael Scott.
21	PETER SIMPLE.	Captain Marryat.
22	MARY OF BURGUNDY.	G. P. R. James.
23	JACOB FAITHFUL.	Captain Marryat.
24	THE GIPSY.	G. P. R. James.
25	CRUISE OF THE MIDGE.	Michael Scott.
26	TWO YEARS BEFORE THE MAST.	R. H. Dana.
27	THE PIRATE, AND THE THREE CUTTERS.	Captain Marryat.
28	HENRY MASTERTON.	G. P. R. James.
29	JOHN MARSTON HALL.	G. P. R. James.
30	JAPHET IN SEARCH OF A FATHER.	Captain Marryat.
31	THE WOLF OF BADENOCH.	Sir Thomas Dick Lauder.
32	CALEB WILLIAMS.	William Godwin.
33	THE PACHA OF MANY TALES.	Captain Marryat.
34	THE VICAR OF WAKEFIELD.	Oliver Goldsmith.
35	MR. MIDSHIPMAN EASY.	Captain Marryat.
36	ATTILA.	G. P. R. James.
37	RORY O'MORE.	Samuel Lover.
38	PELHAM.	Lytton Bulwer.
39	THE DISOWNED.	Lytton Bulwer.
40	DEVEREUX.	Lytton Bulwer.
41	PAUL CLIFFORD.	Lytton Bulwer.
42	EUGENE ARAM.	Lytton Bulwer.
43	THE LAST DAYS OF POMPEII.	Lytton Bulwer.
44	RIENZI.	Lytton Bulwer.
45	ERNEST MALTRAVERS.	Lytton Bulwer.
46	STORIES OF WATERLOO.	W. H. Maxwell.
47	THE BIVOUAC; or, Stories of the Peninsular War	W. H. Maxwell.
48	ALICE.	Lytton Bulwer.
49	THE ROBBER.	G. P. R. James.
50	CYRIL THORNTON.	Capt. T. Hamilton.
51	REGINALD DALTON.	J. G. Lockhart.
52	THE WIDOW BARNABY.	Frances Trollope.
53	TOPSAIL SHEET-BLOCKS.	Matthew Henry Barker.
54	THE HUGUENOT.	G. P. R. James.
55	THE SAUCY ARETHUSA.	Capt. Chamier, R.N.
56	JACK BRAG.	Theodore Hook.
57	PHANTOM SHIP.	Captain Marryat.
58	ROBINSON CRUSOE.	Daniel Defoe.
59	PICKWICK PAPERS.	Charles Dickens.
60	HARRY LORREQUER.	Charles Lever.
61	THE DOG FIEND.	Captain Marryat.
62	NICHOLAS NICKLEBY.	Charles Dickens.
63	OLIVER TWIST.	Charles Dickens.
64	BEN BRACE.	Capt. Chamier, R.N.
65	TOM BOWLING.	Capt. Chamier, R.N.
66	NIGHT AND MORNING.	Lytton Bulwer.
67	POOR JACK.	Capt. Marryat.

Bedford Street, Strand.

Frederick Warne and Co., Publishers,

THE CHANDOS CLASSICS.

A SERIES OF STANDARD WORKS IN POETRY, BIOGRAPHY, HISTORY, THE DRAMA, &c.

In large crown 8vo, price **1s. 6d.** each, stiff wrapper; or, cloth gilt, **2s.**

1 Shakspeare.
2 Longfellow.
3 Byron.
4 Scott.
5 Arabian Nights.
6 Eliza Cook.
7 Legendary Ballads.
8 Burns.
9 Johnson's Lives of the Poets.
10 Dante (The Vision of). By Carey.
11 Moore.
12 Dr. Syntax's Three Tours.
13 Butler's Hudibras.
14 Cowper.
15 Milton.
16 Wordsworth.
17 Hawthorne's Twice Told Tales.
18 England. Hallam and De Lolme.
19 The Saracens. Gibbon and Ockley.
20 Lockhart's Spanish Ballads and Southey's Romance of the Cid.
21 Robinson Crusoe.
22 Swiss Family Robinson.
23 Mrs. Hemans.
24 Grimm's Fairy Tales.
25 Andersen's (Hans) Fairy Tales.
26 Scott's Dramatists and Novelists.
27 Scott's Essays.
28 Shelley.
29 Campbell.
30 Keats.
31 Coleridge.
32 Pope's Iliad. (Flaxman's Illustrations.)
33 Pope's Odyssey. (Ditto.)
34 Hood.
35 Representative Actors.
36 Romance of History—England.
37 Ditto France.
38 Ditto Spain.
39 Ditto Italy.
40 Ditto India.
41 German Literature.
42 Don Quixote (Life and Adventures of).
43 Eastern Tales.
44 Book of Authors.
45 Pope.
46 Mackay.
47 Goldsmith's Poems, &c.
48 The Koran (Complete).
49 Oxenford's French Songs, including Costello's Lays of the Troubadours.
50 Gil Blas (The Adventures of).
51 The Talmud (Selections from).
52 Virgil (Dryden's), (The Works of).

53 Bunyan's Holy War.
54 Dodd's Beauties of Shakspeare.
55 Romance of London—Historic, &c.
56 Ditto Supernatural, &c.
57 A Century of Anecdote.
58 Walton's Angler.
59 Herbert's (George) Works.
60 Heber's (Bishop) Poetical Works.
†61 Half-Hours with the Best Authors.
†62 Ditto **
†63 Ditto ***
†64 Ditto ****
65 Bunyan's Pilgrim's Progress.
66 Fugitive Poetry, 1600—1878.
67 Pepys' Diary.
68 Evelyn's Diary.
69 Townsend's Every-Day Book of Modern Literature.
70 Ditto Ditto **
71 Montgomery (James).
72 Spenser's Faery Queen.
73 White's Natural History of Selborne.
74 Keble's Christian Year.
75 Lamb's Poems and Essays.
76 Roscoe's Italian Novelists.
77 Roscoe's German Novelists.
78 Roscoe's Spanish Novelists.
79 Gibbon's Life and Letters.
80 Gray, Beattie, and Collins.
81 Percy's Reliques.
82 Gems of National Poetry.
83 Lamb's Tales from Shakspeare.
84 Lockhart's Life of Scott.
†85 Half-Hours of English History. *
†86 Ditto ditto **
†87 Ditto ditto ***
†88 Ditto ditto ****
†89 Gibbon's Roman Empire. *
†90 Ditto ditto **
†91 Ditto ditto ***
†92 Ditto ditto ****
†93 D'Israeli's Curiosities of Literature. *
†94 Ditto ditto **
†95 Ditto ditto ***
†96 D'Israeli's Literary Characters.
†97 Disraeli's Calamities and Quarrels.
†98 D'Israeli's Amenities of Literature. *
†99 Ditto ditto **
100 Æsop's Fables. Illustrated.
†101 Hume's History
  to of ⎱ 6 vols.
†106 England. ⎰
107 Hawthorne's Tanglewood Tales.

NOTICE.—These Volumes (†) can only be supplied bound in cloth.

A

BAD BOY'S DIARY

Unabridged Edition

LONDON

FREDERICK WARNE AND CO.

BEDFORD STREET, STRAND

CONTENTS.

iv   *Contents.*

A BAD BOY'S DIARY.

CHAPTER I.

HOW HE BEGAN IT.

I was ate years ole yesterday, an' mamma she says to me :

"Georgie, wot would you like for a burthday present?"

So I said a "diry," cause all my growed-up sisters keep a diry, an' I thought it would be about the figger. So mamma she got me one. I wanted to begin it all rite, so I stole up to Lily's room to copy suthin out o' hern; but she keeps it locked up in her writing-desk, an' I had a offul time getting a key that would fit. At last I found one, an' set down when Lil was out a calling an' coppied oph a page good as I could.

I've got three sisters what all kepes their dirys an' writes into 'em every night after their hair is took oph an' put in the buro drawer, 'xcept what is put in crimps. So to-nite Mister Wilyem Smith he come to see Lil, like he does most every evening, a big, ugly ole bashlor that my sisters makes fun of behind his back, an' I was in the parlor with my diry in my hand an' he ast me wot I got, an' give me sum candy, an' I showed him my diry, an' he red this out loud to Lil and Bess, which was in the room all fixed up to fits :

"I wish that stupid ole Bill Smith would keep hisself to home. He came agen Sunday night. I never, never, never, never shall like him one bit, but mother says he's wrich an' I must accept him if he offers. Oh, how crewel it is to make me practis such dooplicity! It seems as if my heart would brake. What awful grate big red hands he's got an' can't talk about nothin' but how many houses he owns, an' his eravats is in retched taste. I wish he'd stay away an' done with it. He tride to kiss me wen he was goin' Sunday night, but I'd just as soon have a lobster kiss me. Oh! he is so different from my sweet, sweet Montague De Jones. Wot a pity Montague is a poor clerk! I can not bare this misery much longer. Montague is jellus an' reproaches me biterly. Oh, wot a fraud this life is! I'm wery of it."

Lil she was a screechin' an' a tryin' to snatch it all the time, but

Mr. Smith he held it up high, an' red it all; then he sed to me wot made you rite such stuff? I sed it wan't stuff—I got it out of my sister Lily's diry, an' I gess she knew enuff to keep one, an' he took his hat an' went, and Bess she sez to me:

"Now you've done it, George Hackett!"

Lil made a grab at me, but I dodged an' run.

I never see such a boy as I am fur gettin' into scrapes. The hull family is down on me, an' say I've spiled the match an' lost 'em a hundred thousand dollars, but I can't see how I am to blame for jest takin' a few lines out of Lily's diry.

One thing is sure—the rest o' this book will be my own composishun good or bad. I'm disgusted with the fool-stuff in them girls' dirys.

There was such a row to home 'bout it to-day I didn't seem to want my dinner, so I went fishing. It wasn't cloudy, so they wouldn't bite. A man come along an' he sez:

"Got any bites, sonny?"

I wish folks wouldn't call me sonny—it makes me mad; so I hollered:

"Confound the fish!"

And he sez:

"Wot a wicked boy!"

And I sez:

"Not a tall, the fish is in the dam."

And he scratched his head and went on. Just then suthin' bit, an' I leaned over too far an' fell in. You oughter seen me go over that dam an' shoot into the mill an' go right over the wheel, but it wa'n't until after I got into the shute that I thought I guess they'd be sorry, now they'd never have Georgie to scold no more. I don't know what I thunk wen they got me out, coz I was drowned dead as a door-nale; but they rolled me on a barel, an' blowed into my inside with a bellows, an' I come to an' ast 'em if they'd saved my fishpole.

I don't know wot made mama cry wen they brought me home, coz I was all right then, an' I told her so. I was awful glad I fell in, coz they got over bein' mad at me. Lil made me some real good toaste an' tea, an' 'bout dark they all went down to supper an' left me rapped up in blankets that I thought I should smother, so I got up an' put on my best sute—my other one was gettin' dry. I betted they'd scold me for gettin' up, an' I crawled down into the parlor, an' got behind the curtains of the bay winder. I was that tired I fell asleep, an' wen I woken up I heard voices, an' I made out 'twas Susan an' her bow a settin' together on the sofy. Bess she was ratling away at the peano t'other end o' the room. Lil was upstairs, 'cause she knew Mr. Wilyem Smith wouldn't come no more.

"We'll haf to wate," says he, "at leste a year. Old Docktor Bradley wants a younger man to do the ridin', an' he's promised to take me in as pardner this fall. Can you wate for me, my darlin'? You'll haf to haf lots of pashunts," sez he.

"An' so will you," says Sue, an then they laughed

"We'd better kepe it a profound secret for the present," sez he.

"Yes," sez she, "of course. It's the best policy to kepe long engadgements secret, suthin' mite happen, you know."

And then she jumped up as if she was shot, an' run acrost the room, an' set down in a chair jist in time, for some folks come in, and then some more. Everybody wanted to know how poor little Georgie was, an' then mama came in an' said I'd run away—she was awful 'fraid I was dellerius out of my head, my brane might be effected. So I jest gave them curtins a whop, an' jumped right out as if I was a playin' leap-frog, an' the way they hollered would a made you laught.

"Oh, Georgie, Georgie!" groaned poor mama, "you'll be the deth of me, I know you will."

"Were you in the bay-winder all the time?" ast Sue, a turnin' red an' pale.

"You bet," sez I, an' then I wunk at her an' wunk at him. "I knowed honesty was the best pollicy," I begun; "but wot makes it the best pollicy not to let on when your engaged, lik you was a talkin' about?" Then Sue she yerked me out o' the room, an' jis as we got to the door I hollered: "Let go my arm! I'll go without bein' grabbed. Say Sue, I wonder wot made you hop off the sofy when those folks rung the bell! Did Docktor Moore—"

But she put her hand right over my mouth and slammed the door.

"I have as good a mind as ever I had to eat to whip you, Georgie!" she sez, beginning to cry. "You have let the cat out of the bag, you horid, horid boy!"

"Wot cat?" ast I.

"Docktor Moore will never forgive you," sobbin' as if she'd dropped her only stick o' candy in the well. "We didn't want a sole to dreme of it for the next six months."

"Ime sorry I did it, sis," sez I, "I'll never do it agane if you'll stop blubberin'. What did I do, anyhow? If I'd a knowed he was so easy fritened I wouldn't a jumped out so sudden for the world. I wouldn't marry a feller wots so 'fraid o' things. He might get scart into a fit some time if he saw a white sheet on the close-line in the night. I don't believe in gosts, do you?"

By that mamma she came an' took me up to bed agane, an' tole Betty, the chamber-made, to stay by me till I fell aslepe, an' I got Betty to write this in my diry for me, cause I felt so tired and sleepy. Betty's bow's got red hair and a crost eye. I peked through the ary winder onest, and seen him kepe one eye on the cook—that's ill-tempered as she can be—an' one on Betty, an' I wished I had crost eyes, so I could keep one on my book, an' one on Tommy Fuller wen he puts pins in the schollars' seats. Crost eyes would be the convinyuntest things fur boys that have to go to school. Betty yawns like the top of her head would fall off. So I must close.

CHAPTER II.

THE PHOTOGRAPHS.

I've been 2 sick too write in my diry for most a week. It was gettin' drownded made me ill, an' gettin' out o' bed when I was swetty. Docktor Moore he's been up to see me twist a day. He's been so good to me I'm sorry I fritened him that night. I herd Bess tell Lily this morning she was glad I was sick, 'cause there was some piece in the house now; she hoped I'd stay in bed a month. I wonder wot girls don't like their little brothers for. I'm sure I'm real good to Bess. I go to the post-offis fur her twist a day when I am well. I never lost moren three letters fur her. Golly! ain't I glad she don't know 'bout them!

This afternoon I felt so much better I wanted to get up, so when I heard Betty comin' with my supper, I slipped out o' bed an' hid behind the door. I had mamma's shawl around me, an' I jumpted out as she come in, an' barked as like I was a big black dog, an' that careless creture just dropped the server on the floor. Such a mess! The china bowl was broke, the beef-tea spilt on the carpet, an' the hull family rushed up-stairs to hear her scream as if the house was on fire. I didn't know Betty was such a goose. They all blamed me—they always do. I believe when I get well I'll run away, an' be a buf'lo bill, or jine a

ship. There never was a boy got such tretement—so unjust.

To-day I was let sit up, tucked up in a quilt in a arm-chare. I soon got tired o' that, so I ast Betty to get me a glass o' ice-water to squench my thirst, an' when she was gone I cut an' run, an' went into Susan's room to look at all them fotografs of nice young men she's got there in a drawer.

The girls was all down in the parlor, 'cos Miss Watson had come to call. Betty she came a huntin' me, but I hid in the closet behind a ole hoop-skirt. I come out when she went away, an' had a real good time. Some o' them fotografs was written on the back, like this: "Conseated fop!" "Oh, ain't he swect?" "He ast me, but I wouldn't have him." "A perfeck darling!" "What a mouth!" "Portrait of a donkey!"

I kep about two dozen o' them I knew, to have some fun when I got well. I shut the drawer so Sue wouldn't notice they was took. I felt as if I could not bare to go back to that nasty room, I was so tired of it, an' I thought I'd pass my time a playing I was a young lady. So I put on Sue's old bustle, and a pettycoat with a long tale to it, and Sue's blue silk dress, only it wouldn't be big enuff about the waste. I found a lot o' little curls in the buro, wich I stuck on all around my forehead with a bottle of mewsiledge, and then I seen some red stuff on a sawcer, wich I rubbed onto my cheaks. When I was all fixed up I slid down the bannisters plump againste Miss Watson, wot was sayin' good-by to my sisters. Such a hollerin' as they made!

"My best blue silk, you little imp!" said Sue.

Miss Watson she turned me to the light, an' sez she, as sweet as pie:

"Where did you get them pretty red cheeks, Geordie?"

Susan she made a sign, but I didn't know it.

"I found some red stuff in Sue's drawer," sez I, and she smiled kind o' hateful, and said:

"Oh!"

My sister says she is an awful gossip, wich will tell all over town that they paint, wich they don't, 'cause that sawcer was gust to make roses on card-bord, wich is all right.

I stepped on to the front o' Sue's dress goin' up stares agen, an' tore the front bredth acrost.

She was so mad she boxed my ears.

"Aha, missy!" sez I to myself, "you don't guess about them fotografs wot I took o' your drawer!"

Some folks think little boys' ears are made on purpose to be boxed—my sisters do. If they knew wot dark an' desperate thoughts come into little boys' minds, they'd be more careful—it riles 'em up like pokin' sticks into a mud puddle.

I laid low—but beware to-morrow!

They let me come down to brekfast this mornin'.

I've got those pictures all in my pockets, you bet your life.

"Wot makes your pockets stick out so?" ast Lily, when I was a waiting a chance to slip out unbe-knone.

"Oh, things," sez I, an' she laughed.

"I thought mebbe you'd got your books and cloathes packed up in 'em," sez she, "to run away an' be a Injun warryor."

I didn't let on anything, but ansered her:

"I guess I'll go out in the back-yard an' play a spell."

Well, I got off down town, an' had a lot of fun. I called on all the aboriginals of them fotografs.

"Hello, Georgie! Well agen?" said the first feller I stopped to see.

Oh, my! when I get big enuff I'll hope my mustaches won't be waxed like his'n! He's in a store, an' I got him to give me a nice cravat, an' he ast me "Was my sisters well?" so I fished out his fotograf, and gave it to him.

It was the one that had "Conseated Fop!" writ on the back. The girls had drawed his musttaches out twict as long with a pencil, an' made him smile all acrost his face. He got as red as fire, an' then he skowled at me.

"Who did that, you little rascal?"

"I guess the spirits did it," I said, as onest as a owl, an' I went away quick cause he looked as mad as thunder.

The nex plaice I come to was a grocery store, where a nuther young man lived. He had red hair an' freckles, but he seemed to think his-self a beauty. I said:

"Hello, Peters!"

He said:

"The same yourself, Master George. Do you like raisins? Help yourself."

Boys wot has three pretty sisters allers does get treted well, I notiss. I took a big hanful of raisins an' a few peanuts, an' sot on the counter eating 'em, till all at oncest, as if I jest thought of it, I took out his fotograf an' squinted at it, an' sez:

"I do declare, it looks like you."

"Let me see it," sez he.

I wouldn't for a long time, then I gave it to him. The girls had made freckles all over it. This was the one they wrote on its back, "He asked me, but I wouldn't have him." They'd painted his hair as red as a rooster's comb. He got quite pale when he seen it clost.

"It's a burning shame," sez I, "for them young ladies to make fun o' their bows."

"Clear out," sez Peters.

I grabbed a nuther bunch o' raisins an' quietly disappeared. I tell you he was rathy!

Mister Courtenay he was a lawyer, he's got a offis on the square by the cort-house. I knew him very well, 'cause he comes to our house offen. He's a awful queer-lookin' chap, an' so stuck up you'd think he was tryin' to see if the moon was made o' green cheese, like folks sez it is, the way he keeps it in the air. He's got a depe, depe voice way down in his boots. My harte beat wen I got in there, I

was that fritened; but I was bound to see the fun out, so I ast him:

"Is the What is It on exabishun to-day?"

"Wot do you mean?" sez he, a lookin' down on me.

"Sue said if I would come to Mister Courtenay's offis I would see wot this is the picture of," sez I, givin' him his own fotograf inskibed, "The Wonderful What is It."

It's awful funny to see their faces wen they look at their own cards.

In about a minit he up with his foot wich I doged just in time. I herd him muttering suthin' 'bout "suing for scandal." I think myself I oughter arrest her for salt an' battery, boxing my cars. I wishst he would sue Sue, 'twould serve her right.

I'll not get to bed fore midnight if I write enny more. I'me yawning now like a dying fish. So, farewell my diry till the next time. I give them cards all back fore dinner-time. There'll be a row I expect. I've laughed myself almost to fits a thinkin' of the feller wot I give "The Portrait of a Donkey" to. He looked so cross fallen. I do believe he cried. They were teazin' ma to let 'em give a party nex week wen I got home to dinner. I don't believe one of them young gentlemen will come to it; the girls have give 'em all away. I don't care wuth a cent. Wot for do they take such libertys with my ears if they want me to be good to 'em.

P.S.—I bet their left ears are burning wuss'n ever mine did!

CHAPTER III.

THE PARTY.

O DERE! O dere! Wot a world this is! Little boys are born to trubble as the sparks are to fly upwards. It's over a week sence I've had the harte to rite one word in my diry. Poor diry! the reckord of a braking harte, I come to the for consultashun! On this paige will I describe my wose. It hurts me yet to sit down square on my sete, but I will tri to bare it for thi sake.

It all dates from the day I carrid the fellers back their fotografs. As I said, the girls they tezed ma to give 'em a party, wich she promised, so they was in hi fether, an' begun to rite out the list of those they meant to ast, that afternoon. They wur all three as bizy as bees, an' I was bean good, settin' on a chare, a listenin' quietly, coz I was tired, when the bell wrung, an' who do you s'pose it proofed to be but our Aunt Betsey, she that lives to Hoppertown an' comes to see us twicst a yere. My sisters was put out, 'cause they gnu she'd stay a week, an' be here to the party. Lily made a rye face when she herd it.

"Nasty ole thing!" sez she; "she alwis comes at the most unconvynyant times."

"She'll be sure to stay," says Bess, "if she heres about it, and she'l ware that old green silk o' hern, with a yellow hed-dress, and them lile thred gloves."

"She'll mortify us awfully," sez Sue.

I b'leve Aunt Betsey is writch, but she's that old-fashuned you'd think she come out o' the ark, with the animals, too an' too, only Aunt Betsey must a come alone, 'cause she is a ole made.

So when I herd 'em say they hoped she wouldn't stay to the party, I hoped she wouldn't too. To tell the truth, I had a gilty conshuns 'bout those fotografs wich I had done for spite. Oh, it is drefful to hav a gilty conshuns, it ways like lead. I wisht I hadn't done it, but thare's no use cryin' for spilt milk, so I resolved I'd do suthin' for my sisters to make up.

When tea was over, I got Aunt Betsey by herself into the hall, and said to her :

"Wood you like to make my sisters happy?"

"What you mean?" sez she.

"'Cause, if you would," sez I, "please go away before the party. They don't want you here that night. I herd 'em say so. Don't let on I tole you, Aunt Betsey, but jus' go home quiet the day before nex' Thursday, an' I'll be obliged to you as ever was."

I don't think it was well-bred o'

her to get angry when I spoke to her so polite, do you? It was rele mene to go an' tell when I ast her not to speke about it wich she did so quick as ever she could, an' the nex' morning she up an' went away, sayin' she'd never, never, never visit us agane.

But that ain't all. It seems my papa had borroed a lot o' money frum her, 'cause the times is hard, she twitted him with that, an' givin' partis on borroed capital. Of coarse the rath of all fell on one poor little ait yere ole boy. Suthiu' else fell two. I'll not disgrace the, my diry, by sayin' wot—it is enuff to ad they spoiled the child, altho they did not spare the rod. Betty pitied me, an' maid me a rele soft quishion out of a ole pillo. I ain't gone out fur fear the boys would notis thare was suthin' rong; time passes awful slow. I do not think Ide care to be a Alexander Selkirk. When I grow up an' have a little boy I will not trete him so. I will not punish him fur wot he didn't mean to do, but fede him on spunge-cake three times a day, nor let his older sisters speke to h m that rude as if he was a monst r.

Il this time my mind was never esy about them photografs. I 'xpeeted evry hour the cat would be let out the bag wot I had done. Day after day passed by; the nite of the party came at last. Betty drest me n my best sute, tide on my new crevat, an' put lots o' sent on my hankercher, my sisters leektured me for half an hour on how to behave at parties or I'd be sent to bed, an'

I was aloud to come in the parlor The house was all lit up, there was bokase everywhere, a man come to play the peano. My mouth wotered to think o' the is-cream an' cake, the orranges an' gelly, the chickun salid, an' the sandwiches wich was in the dinin'-room. The girls looked awful hansome dressed in white, their crimping-pins took out, their eyes brite, flowers in their hair.

The company began to arrive. All the fashunable yung ladys of the villedge wot moved in our set come —the clock struck nine—the only gentleman present was Docktor Moore, the one that's goin' to marry Sue. My sisters began to look trubbled. I was a shaking in my shoes. The feller at the peany plaid an' plaid. Some of the girls took hold of one anuther an' woltzed around, but they did not seme to enjoy it muuch. Half-pas nine struck on the clock! ! !

Oh, how my gilty conshuns wade me down! I said to myself:

"The trane is lade, the slo-match is applide, now for the jeneral bust-up!"

The gests bgan to whisper, the girls looked like they would sink thru a augur-hole. Then the bell wrung real loud; everybuddy britened up, but it was only Betty brought a card in an' handed it to my sisters. They turned all colors when they seed wot it was. It wasn't "regrets" at all—only a fotograf wich they had writ an' wich used to be in their drawer of their desk. The bell wrung agane—another foto! Phaney the scen!

That bell wrung twenty times, and every time it was anuther, and anuther, and anuther.

At last two yung men arrived. I knu in a minit how they happened to come. On their cards was writ: "Oh, you darling felloe!" an' "Too bright, too butiful to last!" wich was clerk in a shoe-store, but he didn't see the pun.

They got up a set o' lancers, with three gentlemen an' five ladies. Miss Hopkins she giggled a good 'eel of the time; my sisters most cried. The supper was tip top, but I knu the party was a fizzle. I felt so uneasy I had to give up on my fifth saweer of ice-cream.

"If I knu who did it," I herd Sue tellin' the dockter, "I'd shoot him; yes, I would! A mene, dastardly, practical goke. I hate such gokes! They're mad at us now. We can never make it up. We'll have to move to some other town to live. I shall never dare to show my face on the strete agane. I wish I could find out who did it!"

"P'raps George can give you some information," sez the dockter, lookin' me strate in the eye.

"Oh, no!" sez I, "lest it was Towser. I give him some o' them fotografs to chew on, an' he may a droped 'em on the street."

"Then you had them?" sez she, quite awful like.

The cat was out o' the bag. I slipped away an' went to bed. I didn't want to be around when the folks went away. I lay and thunk, and thunk, a long time. I knew I was in for another whipping. I have not yet rekuvered from the effecks o' the tother one. It seemed to me I could not bare the trials wich morning had in store for me. I couldn't sleep a wink. I was detyrmined to run away. There was Aunt Betsey, it was only fifty miles by rale to her house. I'de bin thare oncet. I had two dollars in my bank. The moon was shinin' brite as day. I got up and drest myself, took my bank, krept down stairs as still as a mouse, unlocked the front door and stept out.

I run as fast as I could lick it to the depo. It was getting daybrake. A frate train stood on the switch blowing off steme. I wotched my chance, an' krept into a car wich was empty.

Pritty soon the bell rung—we wur off!

"Farewell, my friends," sez I. "You won't be bothered with that bad boy no more. He's goin' to lye lo till the storm blows over."

After that the moshun of the cars made me sleepy, so I thought Ide take a little knap, wich I'll tell you to-morro how I woke up.

"Who's this?" said a gruff voice.

"It's me, little Georgie, sir," sez I. "I'm willing to pay my fare. Here's my bank with two dollars in it; take out wot you want."

"How did you get here?" ast he.

"I run away from home, coz I'm allus in mischief, sir. I was goin' to be whipped for given the young gentlemens fotograps back to 'em which my sisters had written on. Are you the breakman?"

" You bet !" sez he laffing. " Where do you want to stop off?" " Hoppertown," sez I, " and I guess I'll stay there till I'm grown up, 'cause if I don't my sisters 'll all die old mades."

CHAPTER IV.

THE ELOPEMENT.

I BROKE of ruther abruply las' night 'cause a mouse come out of a hole in my bedroom, so I tride to catch it. I broke my wash-bole throing my shoe at it, but I didn't get the mouse.

Well, the breaksman an' I we had a reel good talk. I tole him 'bout my sisters, an' Aunt Betsey, an' everything. He was sory for me; he wouldn't take money for my fare; he said, wen he was my age he use to be whipt evry night reglar, an' I must get use to it and not mind it. "The frog gets used to bein' skinncd," sez he, " but don't brake off your sister's matches agane if you can help it, for beaus is scarce this year; the war in Europe has maid a corner in the market."

He love that breaksman till my dyin' day, he was so good to me. It was about nine A.M. wen we got to the plaice where I was to get off, so we shook hans and said good-by, like we was ole frens. I b'lieve I'll give up bein' a Buflo Bill, and be a breakman wen I gro up. Such a jolly life ! You can ride for nothing all you want to.

Thare were some boys around the depot wich was surprised to see me alite from a frate car. They introduced theirselves, so I thought Ide stop an' play a spell 'fore I let Aunt Betsy kno Ide come to live with her.

They proofed to be vary wicked, bad boys, wich had no bringing up. They stole my bank, an' tored my new jacket, an' thru mud that I wasn't fit to be seen. I thought wot it said in one o' my books—" Bewair of strange dogs."

It was noon wen I got to Aunt Betsys. I didn't reelize I was hungry till I smelt those puken pies. She was eating dinner all by herself wen I come in.

" Mersy sakes alive ! George Hackett !" she screemed, lettin' her knife drop on her plate so hard it broke a peace out of the edge. " Whare *did* you come from ? Wot's happened to your close? Who skratched your face? If I ain't beat!"

" Aunt Betsy," sez I, " I never told a lie. I've run away."

" Run away!—run away from your buchiful home, your good papa, you dere mamma, your lovin' sis—"

Thare she stopped as if she'd bin chopped off an' kinder choked. You sea she rekolected 'bout how they didn't want her to the party.

"I don't wunder," she ads, "those girls were enuff to drive ennybuddy a way. Tell me all about it, my poor child."

I explained the hole affare to her. I showed her my bleeding scars, because Ide made her mad when she was to our house.

Wen I confesed about the fotografs her eyes sparkled, she was so pleased to think my sisters were in a scrape.

"'Twant rite for you to do that, George," sez she, "but boys will be boys. Ime glad you cum to me. Go rite in the kitchen an' wash, an' hurry back to dinner fore the chickun gets cold."

"Will you promise, aunt, not to let 'em kno where I am?"

"If they don't find out till *I* tell 'em," she sorter snapped, "you'll stay with me till your groan up."

You sea she had a spite 'ganst our folks 'cause I tole her they didn't want her to stay to the party. She stuffed me that I couldn't hold no more, I had to leive my third slice o' punken pie, an' mended my jacket, an' was as good to me as ever was.

Long 'bout four o'clock thare came a telegram from papa:

"I Georgie thare?"

Aunt telegraffed back:

"What do you mene?"

So of coarse they thought I wasn't.

I forgot to say I brought my diry tide up in a handkerchief with a clene shirt an' a pare of stockings.

It was Aunt Betsy's wash bo'e wich I broke a tryin' to hit the mouse. It was funny ole blu china —the wash bole not the mouse—an' aunt felt awful bad. I was afrade she'd send me home.

I've been here two days now, she kepes me jus to spite my folks, but O! she makes me wurk like a perfeck slave. I'm gettin' wery of it. I've had to pick up chips an' even string benes—a perfeck shame! Cook duz such things at home. She will not let me play with other boys. Twict I've stolen down to the depo to look fur my braksman to take me back. He'll do it, I am sure. Homesickness is a fearful thing.

Fore wery, wery days an' nites! How slo time crepes, at a snale's pace. Ime desperut, no money, no frends, the breaksman I can never get a chance to sea. To-day I had to pick twelfe quarts of hukkle berrys, a deggeradation my proud spirut does not freeze to. Oh! could I sea my childhood's home onest more Ide be a moddul boy. Vane are these sad reflecshuns! Stay! hold on! I have a thought! I will not rite in my diry 'cause I believe Aunt Betsey reads it in my absunce.

O, happy boy! at home onct more! Teres blind my eyes wen I think of the seen wen my father brought me home in triump; my mother's sobs, my sister's kisses, even cook was blubberin', and Betty's apurn to her eyes. The hull town has made that fuss over me you'd think I was poor Charley Ross. Thare was a grate crowd to the depo to meet me; such a time! Papa's so angry with my aunt he never spoke to her wen he come to take me home, 'cause everybuddy said I must be dead or stolen. The way I got the money to telegraph was this—she sent me to pick huckel berrys to dry, but I sold 'em an' went to the depot, and telegrafed:

"Ime at Aunt Bettsy's—plese, plese come and take me home. Your son, George."

My sisters are awful nice girls. I never, never will do anything to teaze 'em long as I live. I am furmly resolfed to take the Father of his Country for my moddul, an' gro up to be grate an' good.

The gnu minister came to our honse to tea to-nite. His name is Revrund Nebneezer Slocum. He is 26 years ole, he said so hisself. He is pail, wares a white choker, an' is fond of girls an' sweet-cake, so I juge. He patted me on the head—I hate to be patted on the head, that will do for boys of three or fore. I think he's sweet on Lil, but she won't have him. The only sole on earth Lil cares for is Montagu De Jones. I carried a letter to him this fournoon. She gave me a dime if Ide prommus not to tell ennybuddy. He wrote one back, an' he give me anuther dime. Lil was out in the yard waiteing wen I got back. She put his letter in her pocket an' went up-stairs. Wot duz this mene?

When tea was et we all went in the parlor. Mr. Slocum ast me was I fond of gum drops, 'cause I was eating some. We was by ourselfs in the winder; he wanted to be pleasant. I tole him yes, I liked 'em; when Mr. De Jones give me money for bringin' letters to my sister Lilly I allers bought gum drops. What could a made him turn so green when I said that? At last he ast me how often do you buy 'em? and I said every day. He gave a little kind o' mone like he had et too much. Pritty soon he sed he must go back to his bord-ing-house and write a sermon.

Oh, such a time! Fur onest they didn't scold little Georgie, nor whip him, nor send him to bed by dalite. Pa says he's goin' to get me a veloci-pede next week. It seems I've bin of a good dele of use if I am only ait yeres old. Las' night wen I had writ in my diry I wasn't a bit sleepy, so I went into Lily's room to put on one of her rappers to scare Betty, an' I felt suthin' in the pocket wich was a letter that I read. It said:

"The carridge will be at the corner at nine to-nite—slip out quitely, all will go well; do not fale, me deerest Lily."

"Wot's up?" sez I; "it's most nine now. I'll go and see."

I hung the rapper back in the clost, krept down the back stares, an' reched the street. I doged behind a ash barrel; sure enuff a carridge stoped at the corner. 'Bout a minit after I see my sister Lily come along rapped in a watter-proof, carrying a satchel. Mister De Jones jumped out of the carridge, helped her in, shut the door, un' off they went; the driver he licked the horses like he was in a allfired hurry. I run home with all my mite an' mane, burst in were the folks were sitting, an' gasped :

"You better hurry up if you want to catch 'em. I think somebuddy ought to arest that driver for lickin' his horses."

"Wot are you talking about?" sez mamma.

"Oh, nuthing. Why, Lily's run away with him in a carridge. They're goin' to Plattville to get marrid. I see 'em start."

Then papa said a very bad word. Bess she flue up to Lil's room to see if I tole the truth. I was whisked off to bed, like I allers am when there's fun goin' on, an' wen I woke up this mornin', an' come down to brekfast, there was Miss Lily at the table with the rest, an' after brekfast she sez to me :

"Oh, Geordie, how *could* you tell on us?" an' burst rite out a cryin' I wish I hadn't.

CHAPTER V.

"HE DIDN'T KNOW 'TWAS LOADED."

THERE has been a aksident to our house. It nede not take a proffit to tell who was in fault. I am a dredful boy. To the, my diry, I must aknolige all my sins. I did not mene to do it. Am I then too blame? I wish big folks would stop a calling me names. I am a dredful boy, but not on purpose, it jus' happens. Now the hull town is down on me. Pa sez he xpecks I'll have to go to prison. O, my dere diry, did you ever think your little oner would have to go to jale? O, it is fereful to have the decons, an' the sheruf, an' ole Miss Harkness a frowning at you as if you was a hartless criminal wen you didn't go to do it at all. This morning I was a very good child, I played over to Johnny Brown's an' nuthin' happened that didn't ought to 'cept I staid to dinner coz Johnny's mother didn't want me to, an' after that he came over to my house an' we had a good time all day. We was up in mamma's room wen she was gone a visiting. I put a chair on the table an' climbed up to the top shelf of the chimbly cupbord an' got down some medicine and give it to Johnny wich said it tasted good ; but bimeby he turned quite pail, he was that sick to his stumak he didn't no wether he stood on his heles or his head. So Betty made him drink a cup full o' warm, nasty water with mustard stired into it, such horrid stuff it made him thro it up, wen he felt better. Wen Betty was gone for the mustard I looked in papa's furs an' I found such a funny pistol. Johnny he said it was a revolver, so I tole him not to say a word an' I run an' hid it under my piller.

"We'll have some fun wen you get over bean sick, Johnny," sez I; but he had to go home he felt so bad after he throed up his head-aked.

I let the pistol remane under my piller, fur I was afrade Betty would see it. I wanted to scare my sisters with it cos I did not 'spose 'twas loded, but they would shreke all the same. Girls allers holler like mad wen they see a gun or pistol. So Mister Slocum he come to tea agane. Ministers are the gratest hands to come to tea; it's haf thare work to go around an' take thare suppers with the ladys. I kep dark. Pa had to go to town-meeting, an' ma she went to see how Johnny was. Sue she went a walkin' with the docktor, Bess an' Lily they undertook to see the minister didn't get sleepy in the parlor. Lily she hadn't spoke to me since the nite she run away. She isn't like she used to be one bit, oncest she was equil to a boy for fun and gokes, now I would not be surprised if she settled down into a parson's wife she is that sober, I wisht I had not tole on her that night, she wood a taken me to live with her, she sez, if she had married Mister Jones. Thus one by one my prospects of bliss fade away, this is a sad world.

"Now," sez I, "I'll crepe up stares an' get that pistol, enter the parlor an' stir 'em up. Tain't loded.

O what fun to here them holler. "Betty," sez I, "lend me your blan-kit sholl a fu minits I want to be a Injun brave."

She did not dreme about the re-volver so she lent me the sholl. I rapped it about me, put a cane over my shoulder fur a gun, then I krept up, quite still, so they wouldn't kno Injuns was skirmushin around thare camp. I pushed the door open vary, vary softly, and glared in upon 'em. The minister an' Bess was at opsite ends o' the sofy, Lil she was croshay-ing a lamp-mat, all was still, the hour was at hand, the moment had arrived, so with an uncarthly yell I rushed into the camp, gave three shrill hoops, and pointed my pistol at 'em, saying:

"Surrender or I shoot!"

Bess clapped her hands to her eyes an' uttered screme after screme. Lily gets up and sez soft-like:

"Geordie, O Geordie don't! it's loded."

"Surrender, pail chefe," I ansered, dancing round an' round, pointing my weppon at the minister.

"O Geordie!" Lily beged coming tords me, "stop, do stop!"

"I'm goin' to shoot the pail chefe dead in his tracks," I ansered.

Bad as I fele I almost laugh when I rekolec how Mister Slocum bounced over the back o'the sofy an' scrouched down behind it. Lily got hold of my arm. I shook her off and fired.

Alas dere diry need I tell the more? The ole thing was loded after all! That was the terribul mistake I made. Who would have thunk twas loded all reddy to go of as soon as I pulled the trigger? The ball went right through the back o' the sofy like there want no sofy thare an' hit Mr. Slocum square in the forrid, the ball logged in the brane inflictin' a paneful an' dangrous wound, at leste so the docktor says.

He is a lain up stares now in the best spare room. The Docktor is in thare an' ever so many other folks. He don't say enny thing cos he can't speke, he's senseless. I'm sure no little boy could feel badder'n I do about it.

I wish I had never tuched the ole thing. Wot bisness had it to go and be loded? I'm shut up in my room; I'm not to be let out for a hull month. Ten to one if he dyes the'll be mene enuff not to let me go to the funeral. They nede not be so hard on little Georgie, I didn't know 'twas loded. O dere me! what for dose a little bit of a ball in his brane make so much trubble. I'm glad it was not Lily; she's a dere girl. She kissed an' soothed me when I cried so hard thare was a lump in my throte; I thought I should choke I was so fritened an' sorry. Ever-buddy but her skowled at me like I was a demon. If I ever get to be a man I hope I shal kno better than to pizon little Johnny an' shoot the minister; but I never, never shal, 'cause if I'm put in jaile an' hung I shan't live to grow up. O, wot a thought.

I cried myself to slepe late las nite. This day has been a thousan' miles long. Bred an' woter for breakfas, bred an' woter for dinner, bred an' woter for supper, not a sole to speke

to, the door locked; I must pore out my trubbles now for twilite is coming on, an' I will not be aloud a lamp—no, not even a candel or a match. I am left to bare my gilt in darkness an' silence all alone. O, Betty, Betty, come! Hark, I here a whisper at the kehole—who is there? It was my darlin' sister Lily.

"Georgie," sez she, rite throu the kehole, "poor boy, don't feel so bad; he's better."

"Hurray!" sez I.

"It didn't reach his brane," sez she, "the sofy broke the force o' the ball. It stopped in the fruntal bone, and Docktor Moore took it out. Why, he's a settin' up in bed a eting tea an' toste. He'll be abel to go home in a day or two."

"I wish I was eting tea an' toste. Lily, you a good girl. Don't you ever marry Mr. Slocum, coz he didn't stand fire. Wen I get out o' this I'm goin' to help you marry Montagu, an' do evrything you ast me to. Lily, will you pleze go an' teze pa to let me have a lite? Tell him it's barbrus to let little boys smell waffles frying wen they ain't to get any therselves. Tell cook to kepe the kitchen door shut, so I won't kno thare's ham an' egs for brekfast. Is my squirl fed reglar? I guess Towser thinks I'm dead.

"Tell mamma I'm afraid I'm sick I've got such a queer feeling in the pit of my stumak."

I tell you Lil's a brick! She's got a key wot fits my dore, an' she's brot me a nue book, a hunk o' cake, an' a candel. The cake tasted awful good. If Robinson Crusoe was shut up in a room would he stay there? No, he would contrive to free hisself. If I had some sissors I'd cut up my blankets, tie 'em in a rope, an' let myself down from the winder.

1 had no sissors, but the sheets tored esy. I made a long string, tied one end to the handel of the buro-drawer which stood near by, crawled out o' the window, got a good hold o' my rope, like the folks does when the hause is afire, an' let her slide.

Wot happened afterwords I can't describe, 'cause when my hed struck on the brick ary I didn't know anything for a good while. Mebbe the buro-drawer come out—mebbe the sheets werint tide tite enuff, all I know is that I saw stars, an' then—all was dark as nite. Father sez, when I cum to:

"He is incorgible. I give him up, 'taint no use. O wot a pity he cum to at all!"

Pra, wot did they have me for? 1 didn't ast 'em too. Wy didn't they have a reglar good little boy sent to 'em by Mrs. McCandish sted of such a bad, bad boy as me? 1 guss if papa was kep on bred an' woter, like he was a criminal in the penny ten sherry, he'd tare the sheets up worse'n I did. Folks are so unjust to childrun.

CHAPTER VI.

UNDER THE TABLE.

I don't kno wot makes Susan always in such a awful hurry bout the males; won would think she'd dye if she don't get her letters inside of 5 minnits after the male comes in. I've got to leve off my game of marbles or wotever I'm about, an' go rite off to the post offis—if she's spoiled one game for me she has 3 hundred.

1mo sick of post-offises. So to-day she sent me like 1 always have to go. I was in a grate hurry; I had agrede to meet Tommy Tilden behind his father's barn to buy his new jack-nife, wot his Uncle Ben give him when he went away, an' I was afrade he'd sell it to some other boy, so thare was just 1 letter for Sue, wich didn't seme of much connsekwence, a little pink thing, so 1 thought 1de read it, and if it didn't amount to nothin' 1de thro' it away an' not bother to go back home with it.

The postmaster an' some other fellers laufed wen they see mo tare it open. You never see such a letter; the paige was small but writ all over, an' then over backwards an' round the egges. I couldn't stop to read such stuff. I gave it back to the postmaster to kepe till some of the folks come after it, an' now thare's no end of a fuss.

As useyal Ime the culprit. Just because the postmaster he has a sister wich is a very old made, an' she had the curiosity to read Sue's letter, an' the girl wot wrcte it to her ast for fun, "Are those bottles o' hare-die coming threw the male yct for Miss Hornblower?" That's his sister.

She got mad as a hornet, an' let out she read the letter, and now you never seen such a skrape. She is mad at Susan, Susan is mad at her, they are both mad at me. Girls is always cross bout something. I'm most discurridged about bean a good boy. I shall be awful glad wen I'm gronc up.

I don't think I'll ever marry, thogh. Boys wot has sisters knos too much. Them girls when they come down-stares late in the afternoon ain't the same I see up-stares cuttin' round in their rappers with a little nob of hair on the back of their heads an' their crimpin'-pins a sticking out like horns, a washing their faces in butter-milk, an' a asting me to bring 'em up the morning paper.

I wonder wot they do with all those morning papers? Maybe they're makin' a scrap-book. I've got one —it's nicer than a diry, full of funny things. I cut the pictures out of papa's books in the library to paste in. He does not know it yet. It makes my scrap-book awful nice. You'd laugh to see one I got out of a paper yesterday. It was a boy under a table. He'd bin pinchin' his sister's bow's leg under it with the suggar-tongs. Everybuddy was jumping up —such a sell. I'll do it too. Mister Prim is comin' here to dinner to-morrow. I heard papa tell mamma he was gcin' to try to get him to buy that house an' lot on Smith street. He's such a stick—just the one to try it on.

Cook was dredful crost 'cause she had to get up a nice dinner. She wouldn't make me no turnover, nor let me in the kitchen wen the things was round. That made me mad. Sez I, I'll be even with you, you crost old thing. I said I was goin' over to Johnny's, but I didn't, I hided in the pantry hind the door. Purty soon she comes in with one o' them Washington pies, which is so delishus wen they're just made, all jelly inside, an' layrs of cake frosted on to the top, an' she slams it down, and mutters to herself:

"There, I hope that'll suit Mrs. Petickerler!"

Then she went out. I kep' still as a mouse till she was gone. There is a window to our pantry. I put the pye under it on the shelf, climbed on the shelf, got the pye, an' sliped down an' out. I hid it in the wood-shed, went an' got Johnny, an' I tell you we had a good time. When it was all gone I wiped my mouth an' went into the parlor whare they ware.

"Georgie," sez mamma, sweet as sugar, "you may go an' play with Johnny till we've had our dinner."

"Agreed," sez I.

But I had other plans. I got under

the table in the dining-room; the cloth come down all around; I had the suggar-tongs, an' a fork, an' a bunch of white grapes wich I took of the top of the apurn, an' I fixed myself cumfurtable. They come out an' took their setes, Mister Prim he said grace; he wore shoes, so I jabbed him in the ankul softly, just enuff to make him think a spider bit him; so he said, " We thank Thee, oh, Lord !" I herd Sue giggel, but she didn't gess what made him say it so funny. Mr. Prim is a dredful polite man; he wouldn't reche down to find wot it was for the wurld, an' I tickled him like it was a insect crawling up an' down; he'd move his foot an' jerk like he had St. Vitus' danse, but he didn't let on. Dinner lasted a awful long time, but I didn't care, I wasn't hungry, I'd et too much pye, an' then I herd the girls a whisprin to mama, who sez :

" I'm awful mortified, the cat has et the dessert. You'll have to make out, Mr. Prim, on iskreme, an' frute, an' coughy."

So pa and Mr. Prim they talked about the property. He said he'd take it at that price. While they was a talking,

" Do you kepe dogs?" sez the visitur.

" Nary a dog," sez pa.

" I thought there mite be one under the table," sez he.

" O no," sez pa.

" Will you have calfy o lay?" sez mama, " or calfy nowar?"

" Calfy nowar," sez Prim.

He's frightfully fashionable. Just then I cot him by the caff of the leg with the pincers, an' I give 'em a good squeeze.

" Ouw—wow—wow !" sez he, a jumpin' up.

The cup went smash inter the glass pickel dish, the coughy spilt on to the table-cloth, the cup and saucer an' dish wur broke—such a time ! I know I turned pail. I hadn't meant to pinch so hard, but the mischief was done !

" I'll hav hidrofobia, I kno I will !" yelled Mr. Prim. " Confound your dog ! Send for the doctor fur to cut it out. I've allus had a pursentment I'd die of hidrafobia, an' now I'm bit—I'm bit ! O lord, my leg. Send fur the dockter quick, or it 'ill be to late. O, how horrible it will be to die of that dred disese hidrofobia ! O, ow !"

The girls they all jumped up on chares an' skremed. I wished the floor would open and let me drop into the seller, but it didn't. Pa opened the door to drive the mad dog out, cot up a chair an' poked, an' poked, an' cried " git out !" till he was tired.

All of a sudden a thot seemed to come into his mind—he stooped down, raised the table-cloth, and looked.

" It's only that confounded boy ! Georgie come out here ! What possest you to a thing like that, you little imp ! I'm very angry with you. Come out here ! Go to your room, sir, and remain until I have time to attend to your case. You shall be severely punished, sir. Well, well, friend Prim, better to have a trick played off on you by a bad little boy, than to have hidrafobia, eh? Sit down, sit down. Get off those chares, girls. Wife, pore another cup o' coughy for our gest."

But that ole stick was mad as hops, an' took his hat and left. They say papa's lost the sail, and I'm to blame, as ever.

Wot would you do if you was such a boy? I got a awful licking, too. I fele very lo-spirited to-nite, dear diry. Evrybuddy is down on a feller if he does the leste thing. You'd think he'd committed bluddy murder. I wish they ware all in Halifax but me an' Sue an' Betty. Betty's good. She's brot me mama's camfor-ice, an' Susan's glycerine, an' some salve she had herself, an' a sawcer of iskreme. I tell you wot, if I ever do marry eny girl it will be Betty. If she'll brake off with that red haired raskal wot's a freckled milkmun as wants her to set up a dary with him, I'll marry her as soon as I'me big enuff. A girl that stands by a feller thru thick an' thin is the girl for me.

I guess papa was sorry he licked me so hard, that was three days ago, 'cause yesterday evening he took me to see Herman at the town-hall whare his sho comes off. He is a prestydigatater, a person wot purforms wunderful tricks, like he was the ole satan hisself. You don't see how he does 'em. I watched him awful clost but I couldn't catch him at it. I wish I knew how he did 'em. I b'leve I can perform some of those tricks myself. Wen I grow up I'm going to be one, I mene a prestydigatater, some of them were real esy. I'm going to try the eggs an' the handkerchif, an' swoller the sord, an' borrow the lady's wotch, an' sevral other tricks. The girls will be surprised to find their little brother can do 'em, too. I must practise by myself till I lern the black art, an' then I'll have a table in the parlor, sell tickets to my sisters an' their bows, an' show 'em how it's done. I'm glad I've made up my mind to be a prestydigatater. I think I'll like the business.

CHAPTER VII.

THE LITTLE PRESTIDIGITATEUR.

You never saw such a muss in your life as thare has bin in our house the last few days! P'raps I can ride a horse in a circus ring, but I've abandoned the attempt to be a magishun. It don't pan like I 'xpected. It looks esy wen he's a doin' of it, but wen you come to try it yourself, you're disappointed. The night after pa took me to Herman's sho I thought I'd have a sho myself.

Lotty Sears an' 2 other girls wos

in to spend tho evenin' with my sisters. I went in cook's pantry and hooked a duzznn eggs. There was a yung man cum with Lotty Sears, a reg'lar swell from Nu York, you never see! I got the eggs an' then I wanted a hat like Herman used, so I took his'n off tho hat-rack in the hall—it wus a shiny bever hat, the latest thing in hats. I smashed the eggs up in the hat, an' then I got a little table in the back parlor an' fixed my things so I could pla I was a wizzard, an' then I sez :

" Folks, won't you come to my exhishun? I'm a prestydigatater. Entranse 26 sents."

They all laffed, an' come in ; the yung swell he give n.e 25 sents for the hull crowd. I took up the hat an' shook it, an' said :

" Ladys an' gentlemen, this is the egg trick."

They looked in an' seen the eggs all in a jelly. The feller he didn't kno it was his hat, an' my sisters they didn't think at first, so they smiled like enny thing.

" Now you see it," sez I.

" Yes," sez they.

" Now you don't," sez I.

Then I shook 'em an' did wot the wizzard did, but tho plagy eggs wouldn't come together again. I had to give it up. The swell he laffed fit to kill, but wen I said I was sorry his hat was in such a sticky mess ; what would he ware home? he got serus mighty qick ; his face got about 3 feet long, he looked as if he'd like to eat me. Bess clered me out the room, Sue said she'd tell my father, an' so it gose—a innocent little

boy can't do the lese thing 'thout he's scolded an' banged round. Offen an' offen have I wisht I was a injy-rubber boy.

The next day I thought I'd have a sho out to the stable. I put my prices down to 1 sent. All the boys come in. I had mamma's gold watch —I got it out of her buro drawer wen she was eting dinner—an cook's morter-an'-pestle that she pounds almonds an' crowkets in. I sed :

" Will enny lady lend me her gold watch?" like I herd Herman ask, an' Johnny, as he grede 'cause I let him come in for nothin', he said :

" I'll lend you mine," au' he gives me over mamma's watch, wot I'd put in his pocket for that purpose ; so I pounded it all up.

It was awful hard to smash—on the crystel, that broke esy. I had to take a stone at last. I said :

" You see the watch is all banged up?"

They hollered, " Yes."

I took it an' held it behind my back a minit, au' then I let 'em see the watch game. I was awful scart wen I saw it was just the same an' wouldn't go back nice like it was.

The boys were scart, too, so we hid it in the manger, so tho folks would think that Prince—that's our horse—had got it out the buro drawer an' chewed it up.

" You ain't swollered the sword !" yelled little Bill Brown.

I said I hadn't got a sword to swoller.

" Won't a jacknife do as well?" asked Bcb Smith.

I said I'd try. Then he opened his big jacknife, and lent it to me.

I tried to swoller it, but I choked perfekly dredful—the blood came out my mouth—so Bill he hollered: "Give it up! You ain't no prestydigtater worth a fig!"

All the boys said I'd given 'em away—I must pay back their sents. So I did, an' my tong hurt awful—swelled up like enny thing. I was as mad as a hornet 'cause they talked so; so I went into the house.

Mamma ast me what was the matter with my mouth. I said I guessed it was the blood-beets we had fer dinner.

I didn't feel very good the rest the afternoon. My tung hurt like fury. I felt kind of sorry, too, about mamma's watch.

When we was at tea, an' I dippin' my cake in my tea, 'cause my tung was sore, in comes Sam, rite in the dinin'-room—he s our man—with cook an' Betsy, he a holdin' up the watch. Ev'ry one the folks looked at it, then looked at me. Wot made 'em?

"I found it in the manger," gasped Sam, giving it to mamma.

"Mamma," sez I, "I do b'lieve Prince must a got it out yure buro an' chewed it up like that. Lemme look," sez I, "an' see if I can see the prints o' his teeth into the case."

"Oh, my son, my son, my son," says mamma, "don't you remember the story of your namesake, little Georgie Washton an' his hatchet?" an' lookin' at the watch agane, she burst into teres an' retreted from the room.

"How came you with it?" ast my father, so sturnly that I began to shake.

But let me drop the curtin on the haroing scene, as they say in stories. I will not pollute thy pages, my dere diry, with what happened nex. Suffishunt be it to remark that for the following week my one grate thought was, "Oh, how I wish I was a Edison, so I could get out a patent for making injy rubber little boys!" When I gro up an' have a family, I don't mean to punish 'em for wot they didn't mean to do. Such unjustness is enough to make a boy pack up his nite-shirt, an' his tooth-brush, an' run away an' live with Injuns. Why don't they go an' buy another watch? There's plenty down to Mr Goldsmith's jurely store, stid of making such a fuss about that.

At last they've got somethin' else to think of 'sides little Georgie bean such a dreadful bad child. They're as pleasant and good-natured as a basket o' chips. Montague de Jones' old aunt over in Ireland has dide an' left him five thousand pounds. I'm sure I don't kno wot it's pounds of —mebbe it's pounds of money, which would be a awful lot, wouldn't it? He and Lilly is goin' to get married now. Pa says he allers did think Montague was a nice feller—only too yung to marry.

So it's all made up. I'm goin' to try to be a real good boy till after the wedding, 'cause Lil she took me in her room an' talked to me with teres in her eyes, an' gave me a gold dollar to keep, an' ast me wouldn't I try an' not do any mischief, 'cause everyboddy was in such a hurry, so much to do, and she wanted the affare to go off without any aksidents.

Lil's a good girl. I like her best. I'm going to try to pleze her, so's I can go an' live with her when she's got a home of her own. She sez I may. She'll have a little room on purpose for me, with a buzz saw, an' a keg o' nails, an' a set of tools.

I guess I won't tell Montague she bleached her hair to make it that gold color with tar sope—it used to be as black as cole. O goody! ain't I glad—such lots o' cake. Little Johnny's folks ain't got a wedding like our folks has! I crowed over him to-day, you bet.

I've been so busy that I haven't writ in my diry for awful long time. I guess folks find out their little brothers can be useful when they're ast pleasantly.

My legs is that tired when I go to bed, runnin' for spools of thread, silk, cotton, needles, patterns, raisins, citron, post offiss, notes to Mr. De Jones, an' so forth, I wish I could take them off like old Billy Giles does his, at nite.

To-morrow is the grate day wen the wedding will take place. I must go to bed at onst, so's to be up urly.

It is all over at last. I got up bright and urly. They were to be married in church at eleven o'clock. Cook an' everyboddy was too busy to get breakfast. She said:

"Get yourself some bread and butter; I've got lots to attend to."

I didn't kno boys had to eat bread and butter wen they're sisters got married. I went in where they had a grate long table set, all flowers an' cake, salad, oysters, you don't kno. As I stood up I was able to eat 'bout twicst as much as if I'd set down.

Noboddy was in there. I spilled a decanter on the table-cloth. Such a stain! such a owder of sherry! I got out quick's I could so's they'd think Betty tipped it over.

Betty she said " Come be dressed," so I was dressed, an' had a button-hole boquet, a hankerchif stuck out my brest pocket, an' shiny shoes.

" Sit down," sez she : " kepe still, so you wont spoil your clothes."

I sat down a little while, then I slipped out the back door an' went over to Johnny's to play a spell to pass away the time. So Johnny said, " Thare's a nice big mud puddle where we can sail our boats," an' he pushed me in, which surely wasn't my fault.

When I got home the hull company had to wait while I was dressed in my ole clothes, an' mamma cryin bout the table-cloth, purtendin she was cryin cause her doughter was goin away, an papa whispering he would " tend to me when all was over."

I tell you Lil looked nice when she come down-stares in her white satin, her chekes as red as roses, a grate white vail all over her. Sue looked pretty, too. She was the brides-made. Mr. De Jones seemed as if he couldn't believe it was Ocktober, he was so warm an uncomfortable; he stepped on Lil's train an tore it, so they had to pin it up in the hall; he wondered where his hat was when it was on his head, an he burst forr pares of white kids trying to get them on, he was in such a hurry So I pinned Aunt Betsey's red silk hankerchif onto to his cote behind, an nobody found it out till he was walkin up the ile. All the people began to laugh a little, an the docktor jerked it off. So he thought he wanted to tell him something, an he stopped an looked back, while Lil didn't kno an went ahead. So the folks giggled out loud, and he got as red as a piny.

That embarrised him so that when the minister ast him for the ring he dropped it, an it rolled along an went down in the register, an Sue had to tak off one to hern. By that time he didn't kno one from another, he was that confused, an he went to walk out o' church with Aunt Betsey.

Lil says I shant come to live with her, to pay for that.

I don't care. I'm going to tell my brother Montagu about those letters of hers I found in her lower buro drawer from that other feller what used to come here last winter that give 'em back to her because she was such a flirt. I'm going to tell him how she pads her shoulder-blade an what a temper she's got.

It was the ministur I shot wot performed the seremony; he's got a scar on his forrid, an looks awful sollum.

We all went into the dining-room wen we got home. I guess there were napkins spred over where I spilt the sherry. I like to burst, there were so many kinds of weddin cake. They drank tostes an tostes. Folks was in hi spirits. Somebuddy give me a glass of wine an said :

"Now, little Georgie, toste his sister."

An' I said:

"Here's to my sister wots gone and got married. May her little boys never get their ears boxed, nor their hare pulled, nor their legs run oph, like her little brother has."

They had to hurry to get to the trane ; Bess she throwed her slipper after the carriage ; everybuddy said good-by; so they didn't miss me, an I improved the opportunity to drink up all the wine left in the glasses.

When mamma came to look for me I was under the table, offul, offul sick. I ast her had there been a earthquake. She said what for. I told her cause the floor tipped up so I couldn't stand, an the chares an table was slipping round like they couldn't help theirselves.

Then she called Betty to carry me up stares an put me to bed, an side an side like her heart would break, an said :

"O, Georgie, Georgie, what will you be up to nex ?"

So I answered her :

"I'd be up to bed nex," which was the truth.

CHAPTER VIII.

MISTER WILKINS TAKES HIS SISTER OUT TO RIDE.

AUNT BETSEY she come to the wedding for all she was so mad. She brought a present of a silk bedquilt which she patched herself. I told her I guess Lil was disappointed cause I'd heard her say she expected Aunt Betsey would give her a handsome silver tea-set. Our Bess was named after her, so's to kepe the propty in the family, but I don't kno who Betty, the made, was named after. I'll ast her some day, when I think of it. Aunt she flew up like a hen with her head cut off ; she said if she give Bess a tea-set that that would be enuff, she guessed. She'd willed her money to the Orfan's Home, we shouldn't enny of us tuch a sent of it if a silk bedquilt want good enuff for Lil. She s'posed she'd *have* to give Bess something 'cause she was her namesake, but George Washton never give me anything an' I was named after him. She said I'd made a mess of it as useyul, an' now she wouldn't get a present when she married the docktor. She said I was a marplot. I ast her what that was ; if it was like a squirl or woodchuck ; she said it had 2 legs an' a friteful busy tung.

Thare's a new yung gentleman coming to our house now. It's my idee he comes to see Bess. I ast Betty if she didn't think so 2, an' she said she did. They'd better make the most of him, for she's that old it's perfeckly ridicklus—23 last May. I heard my mamma tell her oncest she would go through the wood 'n take up with a crooked stick at last, whatever that means.

The new yung man's name is Mr. Wilkins. Las night I went into the parlor where he an' Bess was talking, an' I went up to him an' took a good look at him. My, ain't he funny! Bess she made a motion for me to go way. I knew she dassent speke out, so I purtended not to see her.

"How are you, my little man?" sez he.

"I ain't a little man," sez I. "I'm a boy. Did you think I was Tom Thumb or Commodore Nutt?"

He laffed.

I ast him :

"What is that shines so when you laff? Is it gold like that the dentist puts in Bess' teeth?"

"You're a funny boy," sez he, but he did't laugh so I could see what it was shiny in his mouth.

"You are funny too," said I. "What's the matter with your other eye, it don't go like it ought to. Is it glass?"

"You are very rude," said Bess. "Go way, or I'll tell mamma."

I went away a little while, but I come back, cause I wanted to find out what made his other eye not go, an' I stood an' watched an' watched him till Bess said, afterwards, she thought she'd fly.

"Georgie," sez she, as sweet as pie, "won't you please go tell Betty to bring in some cake and lemmonaid?"

I come back agane just as soon as I had told her, cause the more I looked the more I could not make up my mind what was the matter with his eye. His hair was friteful red. So Bess she made a sense to go out in the sitting-room a minute, an' when she come in she said:

"George, your mother wants you rite away."

So I had to go, and mama said it was awful impolite to stare at visitors.

"Then, mama," I ast her, "why don't he wind up his eye so 'twill go like his other one?"

Big folks are very unreasonable to children; 'stead of telling me, all she said was:

"It is your bedtime, George."

Mr. Wilkins comes here every other night reglar. The dockter an' Sue sit in the frunt parlor, he an' Bess sit in the back parlor. Why don't they all sit together? He's goin' to take Bess a buggy ride to morrow afternoon all by thurselves. I think they might a asted me to go along.

I guess I'll go anyways! It would be fun to hide under the sete an' hear what he says, he's got such a squeaky voice. I'll try to manage it. Ide ast Johnny, teo, only there won't be room.

Mr. Wilkins, he drove up, all so grand, with a new top buggy, an' a black horse, with a gold-mounted harnis, 'bout four o'clock. I was on the wotch around the corner of the house, an' when he went in the hall a minute to let 'em know he was there I slipped into the buggy, an' got under the seat, the curtain came down an' consealed me from sight.

My knees was ruther cramped. I fixed myself as good as I could, an' kep as still as deth while they got in. He took the ranes, an' we were oph.

The horse he flue along until we were out of the town as much as 8 miles. I was awful sorry I come along, 'cause I got tired bein' squeazed up in such tite quarters. O, how I aked.

When it was gettin' chilly, and after sunset, the horse he didn't go so fast, he wolked along that slow I thought I'd dye.

I had a big bunch of fire-crackers in my pocket, an' some matches, 'cause I wanted to hear what he was saying to Bess jus' then I didn't set 'em off. I was so tired I could hardly think if his eyes were not alike.

"My darling, darling Bessie," sez he, as if she was a baby 'bout six months old.

My sister she didn't say a word.

"You are not angry?"

Just as if there was enny thing in that to be mad about! I s'pose he thought such a ole girl wouldn't like to be made a baby of. And then he tolked to her a lot of sweet stuff like she was a candy store, you never heard! Thinks I, Mister Wilkins, if she'd boxed your ears like she has mine, you wouldn't call her duv an' angel. These girls that shake an' cuff their little brothers so, never get mad, no matter what the *big* boys do, I've notised that, but I thought I wouldn't say a word, he could have her if he wanted to be such a fool.

"The dri goods business is reviving," sez he, after he'd called her his angel more'n a duzzen times. "I think we might venture to have a wedding sometime 'bout Christmas."

Then Bess she sez:

"I never did beleeve in long engagements, Charles, so if you say Christmas I'll try hard to get reddy."

Then they didn't say nuthing for a minute or two, and I heard suthin' squeak a little. Mebbe it was the wheel. I guess it was. My gnees hurt so I cannot say for surtain. I was so cold an' hungry, and my elbows crampted, I thought I'd scare Mr. Wilkins, so's to make him hurry up.

"There's somethin' under the seat," sez Bess. "O, my! oh grashus! Oh, Charles, I am sure it is a dog!"

"Don't be alarmed," sez he. "I will protect you with my li— Ouch, wouch, what can it be?"

"Oh, stop the horse! Let me get out," sez Bess.

"Let me see what it is," sez Mister Wilkins. He felt around the sete: his hand went on my hair. I bit his hand a little to make him think I was a dog. "It is a dog!" cried he —"a rabid dog. He's bit me. Oh, I will go mad!"

With that he jumped rite out and left my sister in. [That showed how much he loved her!]

The time has come, thought I, to have some fun. He shan't get in agane. The horse shall take frite and run away with me an' sis, then I'll crall out and stop him.

So I struck a match and lit the fire-crackers, and thru 'em under the horse's heels, which went off like a thousand of brick. You never herd such a racket—fizz, fuss, split, crackle, sizzle, bang!

"Bess she yelled; Mr. Wilkins he groaned; the horse run away lickety split; you never see. I was awful scart myself. I called out and tride to get the ranes, but they was down under the horse, and it was dark as pitch. I expected nuthing but we would both be killed.

Rattle-te-bang! we went, miles and miles. Mr. Wilkins he was left in the rode, far, far behind; Bess screaming every jump the animal gave. I tell yu, it was fereful.

Pretty soon we began to come into town, where it was lite. Men run out and tride to stop us. After a while the horse he run plump into the livery-stable where he belonged. Wasn't he a knowing horse? Thare he stopt rite still and trembled. The men they helped us out. Then I said to Bess:

"What for made you yell so? There wasn't any danger."

"George Hackett, is that you? I thought it was a mad dog a-trying to bite me all the time. What was that made that noise? I never was so fritened. You notty, wicked boy! You mite have been the deth of me. You'll get the awfullest whipping you ever had in all your life! I don't beleeve I'll ever, ever get over this nite. Oh, Mister Livry-Stabel-Keeper, won't you take another horse and go back for Mr. Wilkins—he's in the road somewhere, a few miles back. Oh, what a mercy that we weren't smashed into 10,000 peaces! Oh, I shall fante! You bad, notty, troublesome boy; see what you've done. Your father'll give you fitts."

"I didn't mean no harm," said I; "I got under the seat to here what Mr. Wilkins would talk about. I think if I called a girl a angel, I wouldn't jump out an' leve her alone with a mad dog. Oho! he'll have the hydrafobia bad, won't he? Mebbe he's got it a'ready, he's bit so bad! Mebbe it will make his other eye go when he gits fits! If he's going to have 'em, I hope they'll come on 'fore Christmas, Miss Bess—"

I couldn't finish what I had to say; my sister clapped her hand over my mouth, the men they grinned, an' I had to walk off home, 'cause Bess she pushed me.

They were sittin' down to tea when we come in. Things smelt so good, I was dredful hungry; but I had a hevy heart—I knew I'd catch it.

"Perfectly incorrugable," said father, when Bess got through. "You go to bed till I get reddy to 'tend to you, sir."

As I went sloly an' sorrofully upstairs I heard Sue an' the docktor laff like they'd choke theirselves—I don't kno what about.

So Betty she sneaked in 'bout 9 o'clock, bringing me a jolly good, hot supper. Betty is a jewel. She don't like Mr. Wilkins nuther, no more'n I do. She sez it is too bad how I get into scrapes, a innocent little boy that trys so hard to be a model. She says that Mr. Wilkins just got back awful dusty, an' his boot burst out whare he jumped out the buggy. I ast her had his glass eye begun to go. She said it hadn't. She sez she's going to teze mamma to ast papa not to whip me this time.

So now farewell, my diry. I've come to the las' paige of the. I've told the all my hopes an' feres, as Lily sez in hern. Dear Lil, she's keping house. I'm going to visit her nex' week, if I survive the coming ordeal. Betty is bizzy now a basting cotton batting into my pants an' jacket, so there is a fainte hope I may survive. I pray I may. I here my father on the stares—fare the well, my diry. I've got a plan to escape. I'll tell it thee. I'm goin' to crall into the lower buro drawer —he can not find me thare. Betty will shut the drawer, except a inch for me to brethe. Oh, what a goke, to give the guvener away!

If I hadn't a sneezed he never would a found me in the world! Wot makes fokes alwus sneze jus' wen tha wish tha woodn't? That sneze cost me dere, but let the kurtan drop —the seine's 2 harroing 2 be depicted. I've got 2 big bunches of fire-crackers left—revenge is swete—if pa don't wake up sudden an' say to ma "Is that a erthquake or the gudgement day?" my name ain't Georgy Hackett.

CHAPTER IX.

HE HELPS HIS SISTERS AT THE FAIR.

LITTLE girls is a reglar nusance; they ain't no good like boys. Thare's one come to stay to our house a week. Her mamma came two; her name is Daisy Dennis. My mamma promised me a volospede if Ile be good all the time they are here. I shall strive hard to do my best.

This is six times I've ben promised a volospede if I keep out of mischeef, which sumthing allers happened that I didn't get it. They soy axdents will happen in the best reglated familys, so I gess ours is a awful well-reglated family, cos axdents is allers happening it. I hope none will happen while Daisy is here, cos if I had a volospede I could go a mile a minit, which is fearful fast.

One day of sevun has past sloly by. We plaid with Dolls, cos Daisy had on a wite frock an' her mother woodn't let her muss it up. It was a luvly doll, called Flora, most as big as its oner; so I wanted to find out wot made its eyes open and shut, which I discovered was two chunks of led on wires inside its head, but now they're just as cross-eyed as you ever saw old Ben Butler's picture, an' Daisy cride because I made a teenty hole in the top of its head—girls is such babys, gust because its eyes are crooked.

Once she went to get some shugar to pla tea-party; when she came back there was a awful lot o' saw dust on the carpet which came out o Flora's stumake wen I went to se wat she cride there for. Mamm says Ive got to by her anuther dol with my munny, which is real mean I was saving it to get a bow an narrow. Ime told there are no wile turkeys in this naborhood, but Squire Petus up the rode he has a flock o tame ones which wood do to praktise on. I could li low in his feeld unti I got a shot like Buckskin Joe; deac turkeys tell no tales.

But to go on. Dere diry, from what Ive writ wood you ever dreme I had a heavy heart? Wood you dreme Ide bin unable to get through one day of the sevun without my kustumary luck? I can not bare to conlide even too the feelings that suppress my bosom, as dere Lily used to say in hern. Yet Ive prommised to kepe nothing back. Well, we played taking tea and visiting til I was tired, an' Daisy she was mad because I called it girl pla, witch it was, an' I sed to her:

"It's getting late; our folks will have supper in about a hour; suppose we pla poor little Charly Ross."

She sade she'd like it well enuff. Mamma an' Miss Dennis had gone to make a call. Bess she was helpin' cook make poundcake 'cause there was company, there wan't nobody around to see me abduct poor Charly, so I took him—witch was her—to my room, an' she took of her white frock, an' put on my tother suit of close, so's to be a boy. Then I got my paint box an' mixed up some burnt sienna an' painted her like she was a broonet, awful tanned ; then she slipt down stairs an' went out walkin' on the pavement, and I put Betty's sissors in my pocket an' drove round to the frunt dore with my express wagon, an' wen I come by her a walkin' out, I says :

"Little boy, would you like a ride ?"

An' she says,

"Thank you, sir," an' got in.

So then I drew the wagon as fast as ever I could run till we got way out of the villedge in a lonesom place.

"Get out," sez I, "I'm goin' to cut of those long curls so they wont recognize you as their little boy any more."

"Mamma won't like my hare cut," sez she, an' the little booby began to cry, but I cut it all of close to her head, else they wood have knone her two easily, you see.

After that I set her down in the korner of the fence an' tole her she was lost for sure, an' must stay there till mornin'. Then I run away with my wagon with all my mite.

She skreemed and skreemed, but I didn't let on I herd, cos I wanted her to play she was lost. It had been a clowdy day, an' now it began to rain.

It was quite dark when I reched home. They ware all at supper, the poundcake was frosted, and looked tempting to a hungry boy.

"O here they are," says mamma, looking releved. "Where's Daisy, Georgie ? Tell her to come and get her supper, an' you come to. There's room for both."

"O, we're playing Charly Ross," sez I, " an' Daisy's lost."

"Whare is she lost to ?" asked mamma, smiling.

"O, way out there 'bout a mile." I answered, sitting down to the table ; but they all jump up as if lightning had struck the house, which it had only thundered a little just then.

"Be you in earnest ?" asked papa, taking hold o' my shoulder, that I thought I should holler, he took hold so hard.

"Yes, sir ; we agrede to play it, an' she was Charly, an' I was the fellers wot aducted him, so I left her a good ways of, so's she couldn't be found esy. I'm sorry now, for it's rainin' pitchforks. I gess if you go out a peace on the north rode and look in all those fense corners yull find her tho' "

No one et a mouthful a supper after that but me. Miss Dennis rung her hans' an' said her child wood be frightened to deth, she was that fraid of thunder, an' cach her deth of cold a gettin' wet—altogether she made out she'd die about a duzen deths if she wasn't found inimejitly, which I didn't see there was any such hurry, she was not sugar nor salt, but her ma was in a awful state.

"Your a *bad*, BAD, BAD boy," said Sue, a jerking away the poundcake as I was a reching after a piece.

"How can you have the face to sit down there calmly eting cake with that little angle out in the cold, cold nite! Wot's that a sticking out o' your pocket, you little rech?"

"Nothin' but Daisy's hare," I ansered. "I had to cut it off, or you'd a known her by it. You see she is disguysed. You mustn't look for a girl, but a boy, so her hare is short, and she is that sunburned you would think he was a West Indyon. If you meet a poor ragged little fellow in ny old clothes, you'll know it's her."

Miss Denniss she sat right down where she stood. I gess she faneted. Mamma sprinkled water in her face, and cride herself, an' papa he got a lantern. Sue she went along, with about forty of the nabors.

I was disgusted. Such a row! But it was rele fun, too, gust like it was a child was rely lost—as natcheral as life. I had to quit my supper to go along to show the place. It was rite down skandelous the way they talked about me, gust as if I wasn't present, telling each other how I was the worstest boy that ever lived, a allers gettin' into skrapes. A boy can't play a single thing thout he gets into truble, making out I do things on purpose when its allers axidents. Ime gust as sorry as ever I can be—my harte is hevy as led—I woodn't a done it if Ide a known it was naughty. If I shood get Mr. Slocum to pra for me I wonder wood it make me better? I bleve Ile ask him next time he cums here to see Bess.

Miss Dennis is goin' away rite after brekfast to-morrow morning. "She can't bare the site of me," she sez, all because it rained wen Daisy was gettin lost. I gess her hare will gro agen if it *is* cut of short—yu'd think Ide cut her hed of? I got wet goin' after her, too, but they didn't hug an' kiss me, an' make me hot tea with lots of shugar, and give me peches an'-creme, nor let me lie down on the sofy whare I could see all the company. No, indeed! they hustled me up to my room, like I was a dog, an' pa he sed he'd be along purty soon. Humf! I know what that menes. I'm goin' to bild a barrycade, like they do in Paris when there's a war. If they reche me it will be over the ruins of the wash-stand and the buro. I'll slip down quietly to the pantry an' lay in that pound cake an' some cold tung, then I can stand a sege.

Hush, my diry! all is reddy for the fra! The provishuns is laid in, the dore is locked, the bedstid drew up against it, the buro on top of the bedstid, the looking-glass on top of all.

Now, here comes papa, nocking for me to let him in. I'll kepe as still as Bruce did in the cave. I wish some friendly spider wood spin his web across my door, so that the enemy wood see it and think I wasn't in. If he should burst the dore, oh, what a crash there'll be! I wonder how long will one large pound cake sustane life. It would be gust like them all, if the glass gets broke, to say I did it—that bad boy does everything, of course!

"After a storm comes a clam." Thre days ago all was dark—now all is sunshine—piece is made—the sege is lited—for once little Georgie is vicktorous. They said they woodent touch him if he wood come out, wich he was glad to do, since hunger was nawing at his vittals, an' so the furnishure was saved—the barrycade was taken down.

Miss Dennis has gone home with Daisy. There is goin' to be a fare in our church wensdy an' thursdy night. That's the reson they're so pleasant to me now—they want my ade. I had the toothake in my legs last night, I done so many errans.

It's goin' to be a jolly fare. Sue is goin' to take ten tickets in the hand-organ for me if Ime good, an' help, an' don't get into mischef. Ide like to draw that hand-organ, you bet! —then I cood make my livin' and be no more expense to my parunts. If I had a organ and a monkey, Ide give up all idee of being a brakesman.

The fare is over at last.

> " The lites are fled,
> The garland's dead."

The first nite went off butiful. Thare never was a better boy. I wore a button hole bokay, an' sold five-cent segars for 20 cents, witch was a fare prophet, Sue sed, an' she knows I sold sixty, wich was doin' a good bisness. There was a nice young fellar to the fare—he was from the city, an' he thunk he was a Alexander Selkirk, "monarch of all he survayed;" but the girls did not care, cos he spent his munney like water, so they laffed in their sleeves, an' let him swell around like a pecock, an' flattered him, and got him to buy seven pin-cuishions, and ait tekettle holders, an' a lot of things such as a yung man never nedes. I think my sisters were surprised to see how usefull little Georgie cood be.

The 2d evening past of suckcesfly. It was most time to draw for the organ—I cood hardly wate; it was getting slo, so I sade to some yung ladies:

"Wood you like to see my jack-in-the-box?"

They sade " Yes." So I took it out o' my pokkit and put it on the table, an' out jumped a live mouse I had cot an' put in that afternoon—a little, teny, harmless mouse.

I ask the, my diry, was it my fault they jumped, an' run, an' skremed, and tiped the table over, and the lamp broke, an' the kerosene flew over things? Why did them foolish girls get scared at a mouse ? If they had behaved theirselfs nuthin wood have ockurd. Of course, they coodn't put it out, because they had no presents of mind. Some folks fell down stares, they crowded an' skwesed so, an' got hurt. It was providenshal no lives were lost. Ime sorry the nice yung man got his leg broke; he was in such a hurry he jumped over the banistur —he nede not done it.

My sisters got their dresses awful tore. They didn't have time to take the money-drawer along, so 250 dollars perished in the flames. The loss on the town hall is said to be thre thowsand.

Girls is so silly 'bout a little

mouse! Georgie Hackett—that's me —he's to blame for everything. The citizens of this place are goin' to draw up a partishun for papa to send me to boardin'-skool.

Mister Miller's store took fire from the town hall and burned up 2; but I woodn't feel so bad if my hand-organ had not got destroid that I expected to draw. I had 10 chances. It plaid sevral tunes. It was a foraful shame to have it burned—those girls made theirselfs perfeckly redikelous.

CHAPTER X.

THE SURPRISE PARTY.

Papa wanted to send me off to school, but mamma sade, " No, he'll be sent back, wot's the use ?" coz the citizens wanted me to leve the place. The nice yung citty feller wot broke his leg, he is abul to be out, witch I am very sorry for, cos I shel miss the good things my sisters sent him to ete. It makes my mouth wotter to reekolet them. Reverend Mr. Slocum might as well hang his harp on a wilo tree, for Betty she told me last night confidenshal that Bess was dead in love with the citty chap, an' Betty is a good juge—she knows how it is herself; she has a red-hedded bow who looks like one o' those punkins with a candel inside witch I friten her with on dark nites. I should not think she wood be fritened, they are the perfick immidge of her bow. Mr. Jennings, whose leg is got well, he called to see my sister Bess last evenin'; he said he must go back to town tomoro, but he wood come agane. Bess whispered to me

it wos my bed time, so I said, "Good-bye, Mr. Jennings," and went out as quiet as a lamb, but I crep back into the front parlor, witch was in darkness, an' lay down on the sofy coz I was wide awake as a hawk, an' Bess she says:

"Do, Mr. Jennings, stay til Friday; there's going to be a sirprise party on Thursday nite, and we can't get along without you. I wouldn't have little Georgie here about it for the wurld—he'd do some mischief; I'm afrade—that's the reason I didn't tell you til he was gone to bed; it's goin' to be to Judge Bell's; we'll have a luvly time."

So he said he'd stay to pleze her, an' he squeezed her hand like it was an orange. It must be true wot Betty says, they will make a match. I wanted to fire a marble at 'em, but I thot ide better not so's Sue wouldn't kno Ide heard about the sirprise party, an' I lay lo.

He asked her was she engaged to

Mr. Slocum. She said she woodn't marry him if he was the last man, she wasn't good enuff to be a minister's wife. Then he asked her was she good enuff to be *his* wife. I don't kno wat she sade, she spoke so lo, but he most et her up like she was shugar, an' I fell aslepe.

All was dark wen I awoke, so I went up as soft as anything, but the stairs creaked, and papa he rushed out and fired his pistol.

The ball took oph a little peace of my rite ear, an' made me fall down stairs, so papa was sertain he had killed the burglar, an' he got a lamp, an' Sue an' Bess locked their door and scremed inside, and he an' mamma come down were I was all curled up at the foot, an' she said:

"Oh, Lord, it's dere little Georgie! Oh, my sun, my sun!"

Papa he groned like he was hurted. Mamma she saw the blood on my face, an' said:

"He's killed."

But I was only wounded, like I was a soldyer, and I jumped up and sade I wasn't hurt; then mamma had a fit of highsterics. Such a time! My ear was wrapped in cotton, and I was put to bed wen it was getting dalite. I had my brekfust brot up by Betty, but I didn't let on about the sirprise even to her.

Mamma she cride some more wen she came up to see me. I tezed her to let me get up. Wen I was dressed, I slipped out unbeknone, an' went over to Juge Bell's, an' asked for Miss Anna, an' told her thare was a big party comin to her house that night, so she must be surprised as ever was. She lafted, an' said she wood—she was glad I tole her, cos she woodn't let her krimps out now till evenin, an' she'd put the pillershams on, and have the girl sweep under the beds.

Then I went an' asked ole Miss Tucker, who goes by the day, to come, an Johnny Gill, who tends the ralerode switch with one leg, an' wido Robison, who whitewashes our kitchen, and the two Green girls who work at tailoring—O a lot of folkes like it says in the Nu Testament to ask wen yu give a party—witch they was delited, and promised to go, and not say a word all day.

My peple that I invited all went urly. They were all thare before other folkes came, an' Juge Bell he thot it was a sell, because he was up for offis, and Miss Anna she was that mad she put on her bonnit and went away. So the sirprise party took thare cake an creme an music an come over to our house, where they had a very nice time.

Papa was awful sorry, cause the juge an he was friends. He wondered who did it. But I thot wot a pity those poor people went away without cakes or sandwitches like we had! I gess somebudy tole him Georgie did it, fur he looked at me so sharp I thot I wood go out in the back yard and see if the moon had set.

There was a strange cat come in the yard. It was a white and black cat. I said, "Kitty, kitty, kitty!" but it run away. There was an awful owder, so I couldn't stand it, and I went in.

The fokes was in the dining-room havin' their refreshment, so I went in thare. They set up a dredful hu and cry like I was a wild beste.

"O, go away! go away!"

The ladies put their hankerchers to thare faces as if they had the toothake. Papa grabed me by the shoulder and took me out to the stable, an set me down on some hay, and tole me to sta right thare till the party was over.

It was offal mene. I could here the music plaing, and I hadn't had any supper; it was cold and dark in thare, an' such a smell, I almost dide.

Betty she come out thare after a wile with a lot of cake. It was moon-lite wen she opened the dore, so I saw who 'twas.

"Betty dere, I'm here," sade I, overjoid to see her.

"Oh," sade she, "I could find you if it was ever so dark, Georgie, by my nose," an she laffed fit to split. But I didn't get mad, eos it was so thotful of her to bring me somethin to etc in that drery place.

I asked her wood she sta with me, but she was too bizzy. She sade she'd bring me out my other close as soon as ever she got time. In about half an hour she brot them out, an tole me when I had put them on I nite come to the house.

Betty is a xlunt girl, I prise her hily. I got back a little wile before the company went away.

"You musn make frens with strange cats, Georgie," sade Dr. Moore.

They oll tezed me. Mr. Jennings

he wanted to kno if I sented my hankerchuf with Ess bokay? But papa spoke sternly.

"Georgie," sade he, "did you tell that riff-raff to go to Juge Bell's?"

Gust then, before I could anser, thare was a foreful racket outside— ole tin pans and drums an horns and whissles enuff to make you def for life. Evry eye turned on me as if I was the gilty culprit.

"What's up, now?" groaned mamma.

For once little Georgie's conshunce was free.

"I don't kno, mamma, I gess its the callythumpians, don't you?"

You see, dere diry, I had tole a few follers round the depot they'd get cake an cider if they went to Juge Bell's an saranaded the Sirprise Party, witch they had found out it was to our house and come here. You never hearn such a bedlum as they made—thare was about thre duzen of 'em. If Ide knone the party was to be at our house I woodn't invited 'em.

Dr. Moore went out to quiet the krowd, wich gust houled an yelled like demons, so he came in with his fingers in his eres.

"You will have to treat them," he said, "to get rid of them."

Mamma went to get them some cake, the Sirprise Party had et it all up, there wasn't time to bake enny that nite, so one chap throwed a stone rite thru the parlor window— the noise got worse—I was so sorry I had sade enny thing to those lo fellows about the saranade.

Then Bess sade thare was a big

fruit-cake for Thanksgiving in the store-room, she wood get that; so papa sent it out with a lot of sider and his respeks witch they et up an then give "thre cheers for little Georgie," an hollcred they wouldn't go away til little Georgie made 'em a speche.

I was fereful fritened. Papa said: "You've got us into the scrape, my boy—you've got to get us out of it."

So Dr. Moore he put me on his shoulder an took me out. I xpect I was pale, but wen they set up a laffin and a screeching I got indignant, so I spoke up real loud and sade:

"Fello citizens"—like Ide heard papa down to the hall—"we've had 2 unexpected visitors to our Sirprise Party to nite. One come into the bakyard—it was a skunk: tuther come into the front yard—it was the Callythumpians. I don't know witch I liked the best. Good nite."

"You'll make a stump-speker some day, my sun," sade my father, wen they had gone as quiet as lams, an he laffed so much he got over bean angry with me about the affare, but my best close are ruined, they are burried in the garden, I cannot go to Sunday-skool tomoro; I'm sorry, for I prommised Harry Hanks I'd bring him my knife if he'd bring me the Ingy rubber lizzord his aunt gave him —I wanted to friten Betty.

Next week is Thanksgiving. I hope an' pra my close won't be berried then, for we expect to have all our relashuns to dinner an' stay over nite. I shall have a jolly time.

Thanksgiving is the best seson of the yere, excepting Christmas, wich is better. Children are very fond of Christmas. I kno somethin' about it that is not true, but I shant let on.

Thare are a good menny things in mince-pies you wouldn't think wen you ete them—mete, apple, suet, razons, sitron, brandy, nutmeg, cinmon, pufpaste—an' some has snuff. Cook let me see her make them. I had Johnny's grandmothcr's snuff-box, which I borrowed without her knowing it. It looked so much like cinmon, I put it all in wen cook was in the pantry. I hope it is good in pies.

This has ben a busy day. Bess took me out in the country with her to spend the afternoon. Thare was a boy thare, and lots and lots of hickory nuts in the woods, and cows. We picked up all we wanted. Ile told me about snakes—how they put on a new suit. It is wonderful. I wore my old one cos I was goin' nutting, an' my other was berried. For once I can close the, my diry, without any sadning axdent to mar thy page. I was told I was a very polite child.

Bess belongs to an archery club in our village. She took her bow an arrow out so as to shoot in the country where there was lots of room. When she was tired of it me an' the other boy we borrowed it.

Bess let us have it if we woodn't shoot tored the house, or at any living thing. We went in the pasture, and we put up a nooscpaper on a big tree for a target; but those plagy cows they kep a walkin' about, and most evry time we took ame at the noospaper they would frisk their tales and walk slowly past that tree like they was possest, thare want no utther place to promennid but that. Finally one o' them arrows hit the boy's father's best Aldernay cow strate in the eye, wot just lade down, kicked once, an' give up the ghost.

I'm afrade, wen the cow don't go to the barnyard to get milked, his father will not think George Hackett is such a polite little fello; but I did not mean to—no indede! I did not ame at a single thing but the noosepaper, and if that fool cow would kepe walking past whose fault was it —hers or mine?

CHAPTER XI.

HE GOES TO CHURCH.

Sometimes docktor Moore lets me come to his offis an' play a spell. His offis is on mane street; he keeps a fast horse and a sulky, but he won't leve me alone thare cos thare is so much poyson medicine around. Yesterday he was called out very sudin—a man had a phit—so he sade: "Georgie, you remane in that chare till I return."

I sat still til I yawnd like my head would come of, then old Miss Baxter she came in and she looked at me sharp thru her speeks an' asked me whare the docktor was.

"A man's got a phit—can I do anything for you, mam?" I replide, vary polite.

"*You*, George Hackett," says she in a high-up, squeky voice. "You could pizon me if I was fool enuff to let you. All I want is a little fissic, an' I ain't goin' to pay no dollar for it, ether."

An' she looked all about at the bottles an' things—she's sade to be offal stingy, a perfeck miser—an' she spide a box of sedletz powders, an' walked rite up an' helped herself to a blue one an' a white one, an' put five cents down on the tabul.

Thare was some tumblers an' some ice-water on the tabul, an' some shugar in a jar. I asked her should I mix the powders. She thot she'd get the shugar for nothin' so she sade I might. I made it vary sweet in 2 tumblers, and told her to drink the blue one first and then the uther, witch she did as she was told. In about a minit she had a phit, also— O, a offul phit! I can't immadgin wot it was give it to her—the powders were all rite. She fell rite down, she was black in the face like she had swollered ink; she seemed to be chokin' to deth. I run out in the street to find the docktor—he was nowhare to be scene. I told some folks old Miss Baxter was dyin' in our offis, an' they rushed in an' pikked her up in a xosted condishun an' put her on the lounge; her specks were broke, her dress burst open, the teres were streming out of her eyes as if she were at a funral.

They asked her wot was the matter; she sade she did not take it rite—she gessed the spontanyous combustshun had all taken plaice in her stummick instid of in the tumbler, witch I suppose it had. She pade 5 cents for her sedletz powder, but it cost her 50 for another pare of specks; she did not make as much as she ment to. She shook her old green umbrella at me wen she left, as if I was to blame —wot made her try to chete the docktor?

Thare was a drawer under the tabul witch had a nice morocko box in it. I thot there was juelry in it, but it proved to be a lot of quere little knives an' things.

They were gust as sharp as they could be; so a little girl came in crying that had 25 cents and a sliver in her hand. I expect she had been sliding down a sellar dore. I told her to wate, the docktor wood be back very soon; but she sade it hurted offal, an' I tole her: "Wood she kepe still if I cut it out;" but the littul booby didn't kepe still. She gumped gust at the rong time, an' made me cut a dredful gash clere acrost her band. If she had a kep quite it nede not happened.

The blood got all over the new carpet, so I told her to run home quick an' get her mamma to tie it up. It was gettin' late, an' I was that hungry I couldn't wate for the docktor to see the spots on the carpet when he got back. Yet if I went away I was afrade "theves might brake thro' an' steal," so I lugged his skeleton out of a closet and set it in his chare, an' put a surgcal instrument into his hand. Then I got some fosforus out of a bottal, and made some eyes on paper, an' put 'em in its skul. It was a hidyous objeck, you bet—enuff to fritin any burgler—so I wasn't afrade to leve the offis in the skeleton's care, an' I came home to supper.

Now the docktor says I shan't tend offis for him agane, coz old Miss Baxter is mad, an' Emmeline Elder is down with brane-fever gust coz she run in kwick for some cloroform for nurolagy, an' seen that ded feller sittin' in his bones with his eyes glaring, coz it was gettin' dark in thare, an' she gave a screech and fanted away.

Wen she come 2 she was all alone with the skelton, so she gave anuther screech an' went oph the handle agane; then the docktor came and brot her to, but she's gone into a fever, hollerin' all the time; but they nede not blame me. I put it up to fritin burglurs, not girls, wich was all rite.

I forgot to menshun the boy who come in with the toothake. It aked that bad he coodn't stand it while I was gettin' the skelton out the closet, so he helped me fix it, an' I gave him the cloroform bottle to smell out of, and he smelt it, and while he was doing it I told him to pore a lot on his hankercher—it would ease his pane.

He gust lade back an' let the bottle drop. It broke of coarse, an' then he woodn't answer me when I asked him if his tooth aked now, so I came home an' left him thare coz the offis was that strong of cloroforni I had to go away. He and Emmeline was both thare, unconshus, when the docktor arriv.

Ime sorry the bottle broke, coz the stuff was worth 3 dollars, and the boy most dide; but I hope his toothack stoped. I should not thought Emmeline wood been scared at a objeck put up to scare robbers.

Docktor Moore he says thare must a been a burglur come in after all, coz is gar of gum-drops is gone; but little Johnny an' me knoes whare that is out behind the barn.

Tomoro is Thanksgiving; but Ime not to have a single peace of pie the hull day, cos Johnny's grandmother's snuff made a nasty mess of our mince-mete, so we throed away all we baked.

Thare's lots of appul an' punkin-pie, but Ime not to get any. I think it is rele mene. Ime partiklarly fond of pie. My sister Bess is that set up that you can't speke to her hardly, cos she's cot Mr. Jennings an' throwed Mr. Wilkins overbord, witch has never come to our house since the horse run away. Dere Lil came home to nite to spend to-moro with us. She asked was I as bad as ever, cos she'd like to take me home with her to stay a week.

I wood dearly love to go. Why did they every I set up to say I was a bad, bad boy? We ar all libul to make mistakes. I make a fu, like other folks. Am I wickud cos I didn kno' snuff wood spoil mince-pie, or that old Miss Baxter wood fizz like a 4 o' July catherine-wheel if she didn't mix her drinks before she swolloed them? A fello has to find out for hisself by bitter experience a grate menny things.

Lil says I shal go home with her if I brake every nick-nak she's got; she always was a brick; she knows little boys has there trubles like other folks.

Dere diry, in thy pages I sollumly resolve to be a good boy to-moro as ever was, so as to get to go back with Lil. One day shall pass over little Georgie's head in peace an' quiet; he will go to church in the forenoon, in the afternoon he will rede in THE SUNDAY LIBRARY; he will kepe his close note an' be a perfick little gentleman like he is told.

Aunt Betsey is here, 2. Papa rote her a letter asking her to make up an' be friends an' share our Thanksgiving turkey—so here she is; she gave me a gold dollar when she came, an' Mr. Jennings is coming out from the city to dinner, to—he is 1 of our family now; Bess says she wants her aunt to see him—she is thinking about that solid silver tea-set. Lil brot me a funny toy; it is Chinese; it is pinned up in a little peace of cloth; you take the pin out suddin an' out jumps somethun black, like a snaik, half way crost the room. I've fritened cook an' everybody with it; it makes them holler it jumps out so kwick. Montagu brought me a lot of candy that I don't fele as if I could ete any dinner to-moro. I like him ever so much. He wants me to go back with them.

Thanksgiving has come an' gone. I am not to go home with my married sister. The teres in my eyes makes me rite this crooked, so you must excuse it, dere diry. I got up urly and tride very hard to be a prize boy like them you rede of.

After brekfust I took over some of my candy to little Johnny. His mother has a baby witch came there about two weeks ago; I gave it a shugar-plum when the nurse wasn't looking cos it et so funny it made us laff, but the little simplon tride to swaller it before it chude it, witch made it choke so that dredful nurse had to stand it on its head an' its mother made me go strate home.

I went down town to buy somethun' with my gold dollar, but the stores was clozed, so I bought Pat Finegan's bull-pup witch was 2 dollars, I ode him the uther.

It was time to go to church when I got home. I hided my dog in the stabul, an' went along beside of Lil, who looked that pritty, an' wore a elegant dress, that I was proud of her.

Mr. Slocum preched a ufful long sermon, that made me slepy and hungry. I wish I had not taken my Chinese toy to church in my pokkit, coz I was so tired I took it out on the sly gust to see if it was all rite, an' the pin come out suddin by axdent, and fore I new it that long black thing flue rite out in church,

an' struck Mr. Slocum slap acrost the nose wile his eyes was shut saying a prayer. Then it tumbled down into the quire, an' wiggled around like it was alive.

The yung ladies who sing in the quire thought it was a snaik. They gumped up on their seats—such a sceen in church was perfeckly disgraceful. When they saw what it was, one came forwud very sollum, wiping his spektikels, an' says he :

" This wicked, shameless purson, who can play a goke like this in the sankuerry, is 2 depraved to kno' how bad he his. Such outragus conduck is too lo' for us to notiss—let us sing."

I felt as if I wood sink thru the flore, coz all the peple looked at me as if they gnu who did it. I dropped the hymn book I hurrid so to find the hymn, an' when I stooped to pick it up, the pistol Pat Finegan lent me to see if I wood like to buy it, fell out my tuther pokkit and ixploded.

Such a rackit ! Papa took me by the sholder, an' led me down the isle out into the graveyard, an' he set me down hard on a toomb-stone, an' sade :

" George Hackett, yure a heavy cross to bear. Yure a skandal to yure frends. Ime at my wits end to kno' what to do with you," and he walked up an' down an' groned, like his boots was too tite.

I did not kno' what could be done with me either—I was in despare. Fin'ly I sade :

"I wish I had joined the circus when it was here ; if it's 2 late in the seson for that, papa, may be Ide beter be a mishunary, like Mr. Slo-cum says he's a going to be. Then if I got et up by cannibull, you woodn't be trubbled by little Georgie's offal trix any more. I wish I wood git the mesles and die, coz I ain't fit to live. I wish I was put in jale or tide up tight, so as things woodn't happen to make you grone."

"That's it!" said papa, britening up; "I'll tie you up, sir."

An' he marched me home fore the uthers got out of church, an' tide me in the woodshed to a beam with a rope, and my hands behind me like cook fixes her tirkeys to be rosted.

I could here the dishes rattle an' smell the dinner when they oll came back—time never past so slow. Imimadgin my joy when I heard Johnny whissle in our yard! I called him softly. He sawed the rope in 2 and untide my hands.

"Don't let on to my folks, Johnny," sade I. "Ime goin' to take my squirl and my bull-pup, an' go way some-whare whare fokes won't kno' how bad I am."

CHAPTER XII.

HE BECOMES A BURGLAR.

"Hullo!" says he, as ezy as enny-thing, "whare is my little gentleman goin' in such a hurry?"

It was a tramp. He sat under a tree by the rode-side, eting a hull mince pie. I had been running away about 2 hours. My squirrel was in my pockit, but my bull-pup wasn't along, cos he'd gone off when Pat Finnegan called him, gust as if I hadn't pade a dollar for the little thefe—he was a dishonest pup.

"Hullo, yourself," sade I.

"Sit down an' rest, an' have a peace of my pie," sade he.

"Thank you, I will," sade I; for I was rechedly hungry, that it seemed as if my legs woodn't carry me anuther step.

"Whare are you goin'?" he asked, when I had et it.

I nu tramps wasn't very good their-selves, so I thought Ide tell him the hull truth.

"I've run away from our folks, coz Ime such a dredful bad boy they are ashamed of me."

"O," says he, "yure a bad one, be you!" and he laffed. "Wot you been a doin', bub? — commiting murder, or braking into a store?"

"Nothing like that, Mister Tramp," sade I; "but I'm alwus getting into mischief, like I was the worstest boy in the world; so I come away. If I had a monkey and a organ I could suport myself, so my parents nede not bother enny more about me."

"I've got both," said he very kwick. "Thare back in the woods thare, with some of our people. You shall have 'em both, if you come an' stay with us. We have jolly times picking up nuts an' appuls, an' cooking our supper in a kittle over a big fire."

So I sade I would try how I liked it.

There was 5 friteful looking felloes in the woods. I was sorry I was there; but they laffed, and patted me on the head, and said, "O what a brave boy am I!" like I was Jack Horner. Thare wasn't enny fire, nor enny kittle over it, nor no monkey, but thare was a hand-organ, an' they gave me some bread an' cheese, an' we lay down when it got dark. I was so cold I cride, coz there wasn't enny Betty to tuck me up warm; but I did not let them kno I cride. Pretty soon I fell aslepe, but they waked me up, and sade:

"Come along; we've got to tramp it now. If yure a good boy an' do as we tell you to-nite, yure forchune is made. If you don't do gust what we tell you, you will never live to see the lite of anuther day."

No tung can tell how I felt when I herd them horrible words. We walked till my legs was that tired I cood hardly lift them. Two of them staid behind, and we went into a town whare thare was houses on both sides. It was offal dark, and it began to snow. We went into a yard; the men whispered to me if I spoke or made a noise they would choke me to deth—they was goin' to put me thru a little windo, an' I must crepe very softly to the hall dore or the kitchin dore an' unbolt it an' let them in. Thare was a lot of money in that house, witch they wanted. So they got the slats off a little tiny window witch was open, and lifted me up and pushed me threw—it was a tight squeze.

"Here's some maches," whispered they. "You lite 'em and find your way to a dore. If you make a sound they'll catch you for a robber, an' you'll be hanged."

The cold swet stood on my forrid, my limbs trembled. What wood dere mama say to know her little sun was a burggler? I had run away to get a chance to be a good boy, yet here I was a thousand times badder than before. It was my fate.

"Hurry up there!" growled a hoarse voice threw the window.

I struck the match—it went out. I struck another, and looked around.

*   *   *   *

Hump! that bad boy Georgie Hacket has been the hero of the town to-day—even the minister has shook hands with him, cos peple are glad those offul men are cot an' put in jale. Thare have bin about 20 houses robbed this fall in various places. They found the goods and silver hid away in a hollo tree, where I showed 'em the fellows et their suppers in the woods. I will explane to the dere diry.

When I lited the match I looked around and saw our own pantry, cook's aprun on a nale, the remanes of the plum pudding on a platter. My heart beat wildly, I felt my way up stares, it was pich dark, but I knew the way.

"O, papa," I cride, "get up and shoot them, if you pleze, so they won't choke Georgie to deth." Such a sceen! They could not understand at first. Montagu rushed in, the hired man came down out the attic, they had 2 pistols an' a shot-gun when they sallid out to mete the fo. They couldn't find the fo at first, but they routed out the sherif, an' got out some horses. It begun to be dalite, an' I was took along to show the way. They cot the whole 5, so I gess I will not go with tramps agane, but stay at home and be respecktuble.

It has been over a fortnite since I wrote in the diry. Christmas is approaching fast. Two days after Thanksgiving I went home with Lil and Montagu to spend a week. We went thare on the ralerode. They do not kepe house, they board.

"Behave your nicest, Georgie dere," Lil told me, "there's a good menny fashionable pople in the house. I don't want to be ashamed of my own little brother."

"Do they know I am a bad boy, sis?" I asked her.

"They never shall kno it, Georgie, unless you let it out," she answered.

Dinner was reddy when we got thare—a stunning dinner, you bet, lots of courses an' ice creme at the end, and the ministers that wated on the table just as polite to me as to the grone-up people. There was a little girl opsut us at the tabul dressed in a ruffled silk, with kid gloves and a pink sash, a mity pritty girl. I kept looking at her a good

eel, and she looked at me just as much. Montagu told me the little folks were going to have a dance in the parlars after dinner—he would take me in and I might dance if I liked. Maud was the little girl's name. I had a elegant time. She was very pleasant to me, let me dance with her several times. I made up my mind I would never marry Betty no matter how good she was to me. If her cross-eyed boy didn't marry her she would have to be an old made.

I told Maud I didn't think I should ever marry Betty. She looked down at her slipyers thout saying anything.

I didn't do one notty akt 'cept to stick out my foot sudden, wich made a boy fall down, but that was in fun.

I slep on a lounge in Lil's sittin-room, cos the boarding-house was full. It was urly when I woke up. I got up softly and dressed, and slipped out to see how the town looked. It was a large plaice, mutch larger than ours. I could see ships and water. So I asked a man. He said it was the Hudson river. I went down then to see wot was going on. There was a steme-bote puffing away at the dock. Lots of folks was going on borde. So I went to, just to look around and ask the man at the wheel a few questings.

"How soon will she start?" I asked him.

"She's started now," said he.

Sure enuff! the wheel was splash-ing like ennything. The plank was hauled in.

"I want to get off, if you pleze," I sade.

He laffed, and ansered :

"You'll have to wait a spell."

"Can't I telegraf to my sister? she'll think I'm lost."

He was a ruff sort of fello. All he said was, "Nary telegraf," and he grinned like he was tickled about something. I felt the teres come, but I wood not let him see I was unesy. So I began to whissel. I was cold. I wanted my brekfust. I hed no money to pay my way; I was homesick. I gess I looked blu, for pritty soon he asked me hedn't I better go in the cabin; thare was a fire thare; so I went. There wor a lot of ladies and gentlemun in thare. They did not notis me at first, but by and by they asked me who I belonged to. I told them I was carried oph by mistake. They was sorry for me, an' asked me so many questings about my name an whare I lived, I finally told 'em about my diry, and what a bad boy I was, alwus getting into scrapes witch I didn't mene to; and now Lil will think me offly wicked cos I got took away when I was gust looking to sea what makes the wheel go round. A lady called the stuardes to get me some brekfast. After that a gentleman told me if I wood rite a telegram he wood see it sent himself as soon as we got to the city. They gave me a peace of paper and a pencil and I wrote:

"Dear Lil—I did not mene to do it. It was oll the folt of the boat. Do not be alarmed. Little Georgie is all rite. I will be back to-nite on the boat. Plese ask them to wate dinner till I come."

He gave the stuardes a dollar to take care of me, and told me to remane right there in the cabin all day, and I would be perfeckly safe. They shook hands good by when they went of the boat. You never saw such a lot of ships. It was noon. The boat was to start back at three. I got tired when the boat didn't go. I was eting some apples she gave me fore she went down stairs to get her dinner. All of a sudden I thought of Mr. Jennings.

"I guess I will have plenty of time to go and see him before the boat starts," I said to myself; so I sliped of without a word to the stuardes for fear she wood say no. Goodnis grashus! when I got out that woodshed on the street, I thought thare must be a fire—such a crowd! I went acrost the rode an' looked up at all the sines for Mr. Jennings' name, but I did not see it, so I asked a man wood he plese tell me whare Mr. Jennings lived?

"Don't kno, bub—ask one o' the cops," was his repli.

I went on a spell, then I saw a baker's shop, an' I went in an' asked for some donuts.

"How many?" sade the woman.

"Bout 9," sade I.

So I thanked her very polite, an' was going out, when she scremed enuff to friten a bear.

"Where's your money, you little skamp?"

So I told her I was lost and had none, and I lade the donuts back, an' went out feeling real sad. I asked evreybudy that wood stop long enuff whare the boat was, and whore Mr. Jennings lived.

You never saw such a ignorant set! Not i could tell me. I saw on a steeple that it was 4 o'clock, and I began to cry, coz my legs felt like they was Weston's legs. A grate big man in a blue coat took hold my sholder.

" Yung man, wot's the matter ?"

" O, sir," sade I, " I wish I hadn't got on the boat, an' I wish I hadn't got offen the boat, and I wish folks in the city wasn't such a ignorant set. They can't tell a poor little lost boy where Mr. Jennings lives. Ime little Georgie Hackett, sir, who is alwus in hot water, but it isn't my fault. If the boat hadn't come away before I nu it, I wouldn't a got lost. I didn't menc to."

" Well, Georgie," says he, " if you are lost we must try and find you."

He was a very good man to me, only he was a sort of inquisitive. He asked me so many questions I could hardly ete my supper. Folks in the city ete in their sellers—such a dirty habit!

That nite I was sound a slepe in a bunk—such a funny bed, like a box ! Somebody woke me up sobbing like their heart would brake. I set up and rubbed my eyes.

" O, you notty, notty, darling boy," cride Lil.

She was quite pail, an' her eyes were red. Montagu was there to. They had come down on the trane after the boat had got back without me on board. I asked her was Maud sory I was lost; did they wait dinner; wot was she crying about? She sade she was crying cos she had found me at last.

I told her she was a dear old goose. She might have some reason to cry if she had not found me, but now I was all rite—not to tell the folks at home Ide got into another scrape ; I didn't menc to. So I shook hands with the big gentleman in the blue coat, and invited him to come and see me some day, and Montague he took us to 5 Avenue to spend the rest of the nite; but I've told Lil (confidentially) I don't blieve Mr. Jennings is as mutch of a felloe as Bess thinks he is, else the people of New York would a knone more about him.

CHAPTER XIII.

THE LAST STRAW.

I AM fond of most all sesons of the year, specially Chrismus, witch is jolly jenerally. Cook is that cross with fring donuts, making frute cakes, stuffing fowls, a boy can't take a bunch of raisins or a little stik o' cinmon 'thout she snaps him up like she was a fire cracker. She won't allow me to play marbles with the nutmegs, nor lick the spoons she sturs her cake with, nor grate my chunk of chalk on her nu grater, nor have a bit of fun in the kitchen. I have to kepe out of it all the time—it smells so delishus, its hard on a boy.

Bess and Sue they are going to reseve calls on New Yeres. They say its an offul lot of trubble to reseve calls all day, an' have pikkled oysters, an' coffy, an' cold turkey, an' cake, an' ware their new silks. I think Ide better tell sum of the felloes to tell the rest to stay away, coz my sisters say its to much trubble.

Ive had a wate on my mind for moren a weke. Ive been up stares an' down. Yisterdy I tride to climb up on the roof to look down the chimbly, but it was so slipery I nerely rolled off and killed myself, so I had to give it up. Ive carefully xamined the grate in mamma's room. For the life of me I cant see how the old feller can come down such a smal place. If he should get stuck it wood be a sad axdent.

I wish I knew what he intends bringing me. I know wot my sisters is going to give me, for I looked in a box under a nuther box in the closet of their room, an' I saw a pair of slippers about my size, and some hankerchers with G. H. on 'em, and an offal cute riting-desk; so I told Docktor Moore, confidenshaly, Sue was embroidering him the loveliest smoking gacket he ever saw, cos I peked through the kehole and saw her do it. He sade:

"Yure a sad roge, George."

But I am not sad xcept when papa says, "Go up to yure room, sir, an' wate til I come." That makes me sollum.

Ime a little sad, too, about Santa Claus not bein' abul to squeeze down our chimbly. Its a wate on my mind. I cannot shake it off. I asked papa to-day woodn't he have the masons come an' make it larger, but he shook his head. He sade he gessed Old Santa nu enuff to take care of himself.

I think it would be a sell if the poor old felloe got cot—so manny uther children wood be dispointed in those houses whare he had not been. Ive looked up our chimbly, and I believe if a fu bricks wur out he could slip thru as esy as anything to our house.

Chrismus wasn't a very nice day to our house; not so nice as I expected. I was sick in bed all day, and for three days afterwards. Mama was sick to. Mebbe I got a good many presents. I don't exactly kno. Things was sort of confused that day.

It seems we had a axdunt to our house on Chrismus Eve. It was about nine o'clock. Lil an' Montagu, and Mr. Jennings, an' evrybody was in the parlor; we had nuts, an' appuls, an' cake, an' mama sade Ide better go to bed fore long, coz if Santa Claus came and found me up he'd go away again; so I went upstares like a snale, I wasn't slepy any more than Mr. Jennings was.

Bout five minuts after I reched the top of the stares thare was a vary loud noise indede like the wurld was comin' to an end—somethin' hit me on the head that hurt terribul—they say I didn't kno a thing for more'n six ours. It seemed the chimbly in mamma's room had flue into a thousand peaces, an' one of the bricks had hit me on the side of the head—it is a mersy I was not killed, fur the reck is compleet. Evry pane of glass is broken, the miror is shatered, the cealing has fallen down, the carpet is wet whare the water-pipe burst. We can not have a fire except in the kitchun. The frite made mama ill. Papa says it is a wonder the hull house was not bursted up. When I came to they wur wundering what had made it.

I sade p'raps Santa Claus had a bunch of fire-crackers in his bag, an' they went off. Docktor Moore said: " Yes, that must be it."

Then papa he sade :
" George, what did you put gunpowder in the chimbly fur ?"
I cride :
" O, papa. I did not mene to—I rely did not mene to. I only put in bout a teacupful, just enuff to blo' out three or fore bricks to make it big enuff. Was thare anything rong about that, papa ?"
" O, no, George," says he, vary sarkastic, " nothing at all. Repares won't cost more'n 300 dollars, an', of coarse, you don't mind mamma's bein' sick an' the loss of your Chrismus gifts." I've been vary lo-spirited sinse he sade that. Ime a dredful expense to the family ; its uncomforable having fellows at work this cold weather ; and, worst of all, I've lost my presunts that Ive ben looking forward to fur wekes. By the remarks some peple make I rely beleve they wish I had ben blone up rite thru the roof for good and all. Papa says he won't be abul to get his inshurance renude in this town, he will have to go to the city whare they don't kno' about me. Grone-up peple are that unreasonable they xpect childrun to kno' things fore they have found out.

Jimmy Blake he come to see me to-day an' he told me I need not have made the chimbly any biger because Santa Claus was only papa and mama after all, so I asked Sue—she said Jimmy was a humbug. He showed me the new knife he got; I went to see if it was rele sharp an' I cut a hole in the bedspred, but Betty promised me she'd darn it.

My sisters is very ankshus to get the house repared before New Years.

I don't think they nede fret about it, coz I told the yung gentlemun down to the post-offis the day before Chrismas they had better not call—it was a much trubble. I like to save my sisters all the trubble I can. The bump on my head is sloly subsiding.

Docktor Moore says I may go out doors tomoro. There is xlent slaying—the snow is a foot deep—oll the girls an' felloes are having a hi time; the bells are jingling. I'm fereful sorry I lost my sled when the chimbly blew up. Nite after next thare's going to be a donashun party to the minister's—not Mr. Slocum, tother one. They think it will be a good one, because the rodes are splendid, and it is the hollyday seson. The minister's wife she came to see how my head was; she an' mama talked about the donashun; I heard her say, sorter laffin, she hoped some buddy wood bring a box of starch, coz she was out, an' her husband liked his collars stiff. I gess lle go doun strete in the morning an' let Mr. Peters kno' about the starch—he keeps a grosry.

Dere diry, good-by, I'm off—my trunk pakked. Betty and mama have cride till there eyes is red. Ime going away to school about 100 miles to a plaice witch it says:

"A helthy home in the country for a fu little boys; terms reasonbul; good tabul, careful traneing."

I pity them whare I am going, coz I'm such a monster my sisters are frantic. My father says I am a nuisance—a first-class nuisance, but Betty says it is a burning shame to send away a poor, florn little child to boarding-school.

Our folks woodn't let me go to the donashun party—I tezed to go, coz I wanted to see what evry buddy wood bring, it wood be such fun, so I went by myself fore they started. The minister had gust got through supper when I came there, but they let me stay. So Mr. Peters he came and he brought starch. Mr. Blakeland came, and he brought starch. Mr. Jones brought starch. Mr. Robison brought starch. Evry buddy brought starch. There were 18 boxes of starch and several pound packages. First the minister's folks they smiled, but when it kep coming they got mad, and by-in-by he said very sollum:

"If this is a joke, my friends, it is a poor one."

And then the whole crowd looked over at me, whare I was examining a fotograf album, and sade:

"Georgie told us so."

I only did it coz I herd her say she wanted some. I thought I'd make 'em bring enough. I don't think I ought to be took by the ere an' told to go home before the refreshments. Some folks wood be glad to have it to make corn-starch puddings with. Ime discurridged trying to do what people don't want me to.

So the next day there was a grand slay ride. Any buddy didu't ask Bess coz she is engaged to Mr. Jennings, who is in the city; I heard her say she wanted to go awful, so I happened to be down by his store, and I asked the felloe she gave the mitten to that the horse ran away, woodn't he take Bess to the slay ride? He said :

" No, he woodn't, if she was the last woman on erth."

Bess ought not to have slapped me for asking him, when I did it, coz she wanted to go.

Next day was New Years. Thare didn't any buddy call to our house, the girls were fixed up to fits wating, lots of nice young felloes went by, some of them came up to the door but they did not come in, coz I had tied a basket on the bell handle to put their cards in to save my sisters trubbel. Along about noon Bess took me by the shoulders, and said :

" George Hackett, you've been up to some o' your mischief. Look me strate in the eye and tel me what you've done."

I looked her strate in the eye.

" I didn't do nothing at oll, only to save you the fatege of receiving calls," I sade.

" What did you do ?" she repeted, shaking me harder an' harder.

" I gust writ a fu words and took 'em into the office of the paper like other folks do when they want to advurtize."

Then Bess snatched up the newspaper witch came the day before an' read all over it quick til she came to the speshal notis collum, where it sade :

" To oll whom it may coneern : The Miss Hacketts won't be to home New Year's Day, coz their Helth is delcate, they have a pane in their side when they ware their nu siik dresses, an' it's a offul site of trubbel to set a stylish table, oysters is dere, it don't pay, the young men are shallo crechures any way, they beg to be excused this year.

SUE HACKETT.
BESS HACKETT."

Sue, she was looking over Bess's sholder ; both my sisters got as red as fire—then as pail as chalk—an' sat rite down as if they hed stepped on a tack—there was dead silence like you'd wak'd up in the middle of the nite—the bells gingled joyfully, as lodes and lodes of nice fellows went gayly by our house.

" George Hackett, I disoan you from this our !" Sue finly gasped.

" This is 2, 2 much ! I shall never hold up my hed again ! This is the last straw !"

There wasn't any straw as I could see ; Ide only meant to have my sisters have an ezy time. Girls are so ungrateful, they never ought to have a loving little brother that pays out 25 cents his own money to put a advertisment for them in the paper —never ! I thought if no young gentlemen called I'd have a lot of cake, an' mottoes, an' things they didn't eat, coz they didn't come ; sted of that I was jerked out of the room an' made to stay up stares. New Yeres was the longest day of all my life—if the cat had not come in where I was I beleve I should have gone insane ; cats ain't all the time telling a little boy he is horrid, so I gess Miss Bess will be surprised when she opens her bonnet-box to ware her new bonnet to church to see the cat gump out the box—I put her in last nite.

So now, once more, farewell. I expeck to be very quite in school. I've prommused mamma not to disgrace her if I can help it. I've got my squirl in my pocket, nobody knew I took him along. I wonder wood it make the boys laugh if I put my squirl on the table first time I go to brekfast.

Ilio! how lonesome I fele. That old gentleman in the next sete, he's fast asleep. I wonder if he gumped when I stuck a pin in him wood his spectacles fly off?

CHAPTER XIV.

A GREAT IMPROVEMENT.

How sad it is to be homesick! Last nite I lay awake a long, long time — morin half a hour — thinking about Betty and her crost-eyed beau to home in our kitchen; wile here was I, a poor little boy, banished from the herth of my four fathers, that sick an' wery of the wurld, I was disgusted with the gingerbread they gave us for our supper.

O mamma, send an bring thy poor Georgie home! I cannot endure the way Professor Pitkins tolks about my spelling. I cannot indure the hash and otemeal they have for brekfust. I cannot indure the incults of the big boys. They don't seme to think little boys has any more feelings than a tode. You can cut of a tode's head and it won't mind it a bit. I think it's offul fun—first find your tode.

"Speshal care taken of small pupils," says the sirkular.

Mrs. Pitkins she rung my father's hand:

"I'll be a muther to him," says she, witch made me fele very bad. I didn't want her to trubble herself. I'm not a baby; besides my mama don't call me sulken when Ime only homesick, witch who could help who had to have a dickshunnary in his chair to ete his meals and make the other boys jeer at him on the sly? The way they teze a felloe is enuff to drive him frantic.

I am that snow-balled, like I was a fence-post, it would make Betty cry if she could see them. My silk hankechuff is taken away, my mittens is on the roof, where the cat took 'em when they put 'em over her head. I have not shed a single tear. They cannot crow over me. Jack Bunce says Ime a brick, an he'll stand by me. He is a very large boy, so I have one *frend.*

O, how retched to be far from all you love, just when mince-pies and hickory-nuts are ripe. When I think of three barls of sweet appels in our sellar it seems as if Ide fly.

Mrs. Pitkins is quite a fleshy lady, tho I don't see how she comes so unless she etes by herself between meals. I sit next to her at table on Webster's dickshunnary to make me hire.

This morning I went to be very polite, like the cullored water at the hotel where Lily bordes, so I jumped down off the dickshunnary quick to pull her chare away when she got up, witch she didn't know I knew enuff, and foolishly sat down agane. Of course she sat down on the floor. O, such a thump! But was it rite she should get in a temper with me and say I did it a purpose?

So now she's going to write to my folks that Ime the worstest boy in school, only she's got to wate a day or to til she is well agane. She's got an offul gar. If she had been china she'd have broke.

Ive begun to study geografy. It says the erth is round, but I don't see it. There is a big one in the school-room. You can turn it around with your hand. Ime going to cut a piece out with my nife, cause I've alwus wanted to know if it was hollo, or the dirt went all the way through. I olso study rithmatic. It is a quere book. It tells you how if John has seven kites Charles will have twice seven, witch is too many for one boy, lest it is very windy and the strings get away.

It will be the kite seson in March; but if I am doomed to remane in this place, Ime afrade I shall not have the spirits to fly any. Plane boiled rice with molasses is so discurridgeing I shall rite to Betty, as I prommussed—she alwus took that deep intrest in the, my diry—to ask cook to plese send me a box, and won't Betty help her seed the raisons, so there will be no time lost.

There is a lady here; she heres the small boys lessons. I like her very much, but Jack Bunce says she is an old made. What if she is? Her name is Miss Haven. She seems fond of me. I have told her in confidence how I was called a bad boy at home, but didn't do it on purpose. She pittys me very much. She says I may come in her room when I am lonesum. I think I will go there this evening.

Betty used to tell me Friday was an unlucky day—I gess it is. All the boys are at supper now, excepting me. I am not to have any. It is very sad to get into disgrace the first week you are in a strange scool. If ever a boy tride hard not to do what he didn't mene to, I am that boy. · I have come to the conclusion that I am a failure. Maybe if I were deaf and dumb and couldn't see, I would not have so many axdents hapen.

Professur Pitkins has got a cold in his head. You ought to hear him sneze and sneze, but he's tide it up in a large red silk handkerchef, witch is better than nothing. Mrs. Pitkins is still in bed, but she sent for me to tell me I was a bad boy over again. I wish she had something new to say. She cride as if she had the toothake when she told me she was afrade it would be the death of the professur. I said:

"If it is his death, will scool

shut up an I be sent home? O joy, o rapture unconfined," as it says in Pinafore.

She said: "You are a hartless little imp."

I don't call it hartless to want to go home. It was this way:

Bout a nour after tee last evening, I crep into the dining-room to see had the girl forgot to take the cookies of. It was offul warm an' nice there, cause they use it for their sittin-room. Professur Pitkins he was stretched out on a lounge behind the stove with a book, but he was not reading, because he was aslepe. Mrs. Pitkins she was not there, too, bein' in bed on akount of the time she sat down on the flore. We were oll alone. The cookies had been locked up. I went up close to him to see how he snored so funny. I was not afrade, because he was aslepe! You would have thought he was in pane to hear him snore; you pour water out of a bottle and wistle at the same time it will be like that. Oll at once I saw the top of his head had come partly off. I was fritened for fear it would kill him. I run up stares an told Jack Bunce. He said:

"Shaw! he wares a wig—his wig is slipped partly off."

I asked him what was a wig?

He said: "It's what the Injuns take off when they scalp a man."

I asked: "Has Professor Pitkins been scalped?"

He said: "No, but he ought to be. He's that cross, scalping is 2 good for him."

Jack was bizy with his Latin, so I crep back to the dining-room; the gnifes were on the table, 1 at every plate. I took a gnife an stole up to the professor still as a mouse; I run the gnife around his head like I'd read the redskins do, an took off his scalp offul ezy, so he wouldn't wake up; then I got on my hands and nees an wriggled over the carpet, pretending it was grass. He did not wake, so I got out in the hall, an then I made a brake on tipto for the long room where the boys was studying.

"Whoop! whoop!" I yelled—but durst not yell very loud. "I've got his scalp! 'Fy had a belt, I'd fasten it on."

You never herd such a row as those pupils made.

"Bully for you, Georgie!"

"You'll be expelled!"

"The professor will be offul mad!"

"How dare you do it?"

"Stick to it, Georgie!"

"Less see wot it looks like!"

I passed it round. We had jolly fun. I tride it on; so did the other felloes. Then they put it on me agane, and they put me up on the hi desk, an sade:

"Give us a leckture, Georgie!"

So I put my hand behind me, like it was the professor's cote tail, an coffed an clered my throte, an said:

"Hem! yung gentlemen, I wish to call yure attenshun to-day to the anmal kingdum, witch is all sorts and sizes. The elefunt is sevral sizes larger than the flea, but the flea has got the grab on the elefunt when it comes to jumping. I would not want an elefunt crolling up an down my back when I was aslepe. I will not kepe you long to-day, yung gentlemen, because I kno you wish to go a-snow-balling poor little Georgie Hackett, the smallest boy in scool."

They let me come down after that. Jack Bunce he whispered I'd better take it back; I said I wood. But gust as I slid down the banisturs to do it, the professor come in the hall very quick. Of course I could not stop; the soles of my shoes took him right in the mouth, witch made it bleed a little, an his teeth came out.

It was too bad. I did not kno his teeth came out, besides, I could not help it.

While he was wiping away the blood I slipped into the room an put his scalp into the stove quick and shut it up, for he was in such a temper I durst not own up I'd took it of with a gnife.

The top of his head looked like the ostrich egg my cousin brought; so he asked me whare was his wig. I asked him did he think it was the cat? He shook me so friteful hard that I couldn't help crying; so I sade perhaps the Utes had made a rade an scalped him while he dremed. O how stern he appered!

He sent for every boy in scool. Not one could tell him what had happund to his hed. I suggested perhaps the rats had carried it into a hole. He got rathier and rathier, and then he began to sneeze. I felt that sorry when I herd him sneeze I wished I hadn't burned the old thing; I had no idea a grone-up man cought cold so ezy; so I asked him hadn't

he better go to bed and have a mustard plaster on his head.

He said if it were not so soon after the holidays he would suspend the scool; such wicked boys desurved to be disgraced; he was almost certain it was I had done the deed; he should find out soon, and then wo to the gilty! I thought what mamma told me how rong it was to tell a lie; I choked down my sobs.

"Professor Pitkins, the other felloes are not to blame—it was the cat. I saw her playing with it when I came down to tell Bridget if she had not put the cookies away, she'd better do it 'fore the other boys took 'em."

Professor Pitkins put on his specktickles and looked at me a good while, offul sharp, like I was one of those wrigglers you put in a mycroscope. I felt like I was srinking up to nothing. It became necessary to turn the subjec', an' I asked him:

"Were you born balled, professor? Did your nurse forget to bring you any teeth? Why didn't she give you a pare of eyes war'nted to last, so you wouldn't have to put on glasses to see a little boy of my size? I'm offul sorry you've cot cold, but don't you think you're about old enough to die without making a fuss about it?"

He got as red as a lobster, and fround terribly; I gess he was going to say something severe, for he got so far as:

"You are the most impertnant little ker-cheu—I ever ker-cheu."

An' then he just made a brake an' got out the room, 'cause the felloes were giggling into their pocket hankerchefs—he's gone round to-day with his head tide up—he don't look like a professur. They say he telegrafed for a wig, witch is to come up by express to-nite. The boys have a hollyday, so they think it is oll rite, but I'm a prisoner in my room on bread an' molasses, witch is disgusting.

I don't kno how I could have passed this tejus day only I found a stovepipe hole in the floor stopped up with a round pease of tin, witch I took out. When I looked down it was rite over Mrs. Pitkins' buro, where there was lots and lots of things lying around, so I bent a pin and tide it to a long string in my pockket, and I've played I was fishing to wile away the ours. I've cot a lot of queer fish—a pear of get bracelets, a laee cover ofen the pin-quishion, some fereful funny curls, seven hairpins, several collars an' cuffs, three mats, a bottle of colone witch happened to have a blue ribbon around it that the pin hooked into ezy, an' a box of powder, only the box came open an the powder flue over everything, so I've shut up the stove-pipe hole now, so I won't get seolded for spilling it.

Dere diry, I must rite to mama now how much I've lurned in my geografy an' otherthings, she wouldn't believe only I'm that perfekly homesick she'd better send me a frute-cake soon. I'm that improved in spelling and good conduk she might add a gelly-cake.

CHAPTER XV

HE BECOMES A KLEPTOMANIAC.

It's od how much a boy lurns when he goes to bording-seool. Arthur Brown has shown me how to throw a paper wad so's nobudy won't kno it wus you who thrown it. Willie Wilson has shone me how to get up after you go to bed and have lots of fun; also how to rite your answers down on a slip of paper in your book, so you don't have to study so hard. Mental rithmetic is offul hard—you have to do it all in your head—it gives you headake when you want to go skating.

It's much easier on the slate, coz you can make a picture of the Professor when you are not ading up your sums; and you can draw Mrs. Pitkins very stout, only you muss rubber out quiek before she sees you at it, for it makes her fereful mad to be drawn brodder than she is long. She cot me at it yesterday. I had to stand in the middle of the room and ware a dunce cap made out of fool's paper. I didn't care, but Betty will be huffy when I rite to her how I am treated. I told her I would rather wear it than a wig—she got as red as fire!

They seem to have a prejudis against me here because that axdent hapened to his wig, witch was the menes of his getting a better one. They are reddy to pounce down on little Georgie every time a thing goes wrong.

It was not me who spilt the ink from one end of the room to the other—it is ungust to lay the blame on me, when all I did was to tie the inkstand to the cat's tail—it was the cat that spilt the ink.

The Professur says if anything more of the kind okkurs, I will be suspended. I asked Jack Bunce what suspended was; he told me to look in the big dickshunary I sit on when I eat—it says " to be attached to something above; to hang." O, what a fate for a small boy! I thought wicked murdrers were the only people who were hung.

Miss Haven says I will not be hung, I will only be sent home, the very thing I want; but she says my mamma an' sisters would feel bad—it would be a disgrace—just think of it! to see their own little brother, how would that be a disgrace! But I have promised Miss Haven I will be careful not to do so any more.

She has a bow. I saw his fotograf. I told her about Lil and Montagu, and asked her when would she get married? She answered, when her ship came in; so I spose he is a sailor. I told her I was sory, for if she had waited till I grew up, I would have married her myself. She is much nicer than Mrs. Pitkins. I

think she is not happy here, for she was in teres when I went in her room; but perhaps she had been eting peppermint-drops, witch sometimes makes the eyes water.

Mrs. Pitkins is that afrade of burglers, the boys say there is hardly a nite she don't waken the professur, hollerin out for him to get up, there are burglers in the house. I don't kno why, unless they want to steal the boys. It is a pity he should get up so often without finding one, so last nite there really was one under their bed. He waited until they were sound aslepe. Mrs. Pitkins snores in her sleep, like you pore water out of a gug. All at once she waked up an' whispered:

"Pitkins! Pitkins! there's a burglar under the bed!"

He sade:

"Nonsense, go to slepe."

"There *is*," says she; "I fele him under the springs a moving round. Pitkins, get up! fire! murder! thieves! O, Pitkins, strike a lite!"

He told her she was a fool. Just then the burglar's back hit the springs under him. He bounced out on the flore like he was a rubberball. She folloed, gasping for breath, but she was so unfortunit as to roll out, and so fritened she could not get up off the flore, so she hollered the burgler was a murdring her, he had her by the throte. At that Pitkins rushed out into the hall and called Jack Bunce, with several other large boys. They made a lite. You never saw how she looks with her hair in papers, in a flannel nite-gown, it would make you laff. Jack Bunce looked under the bed. Thare was no one thare, because I had darted out in the darkness, and was sound aslepe in bed before Jack came back. All was quiet along the Potomac. For once little Georgie was not mixed up in the scrape. Mrs. Pitkins has sent her brest-pin and his bosom-studs to be kep in a safe in the village. I hope nothing will hapen to them. It would be a sad loss.

Alas! to think that little Georgie, his mother's pet, should ever be such a long, quere thing as a klepto-maniact. That is the latest thing out. I am one. Yesterday I had to go round all day with a piece of paper on my forrid, on which was writ:

" KLEPTOMANIACT."

That menes you can't help taking things. The way I came to be one was this: I told the, dere diry, bout the stove-pipe hole over Mrs. Pitkins' buro.

Well, they xamined my trunk, as well as the other boys, to find out whether it was rats or spirits, or what it was. You never saw such a mess as they found in my poor little trunk. Mrs. Pitkins' hand-glass, lace colars, bloom of youth, 2 pinquishions, 6 hankerchefs, 1 bus-sel, 1 feather-duster, 1 reticule, with a pocket-book in it, 50 cents in the pocket-book, a pakkage tide up witch she had been out shoping, 1 pare new gaiters; last, but not leste, Profesur Pitkins' silver wotch an' his new wig witch he had to telegraf for when I burnt his other one, witch he was so careless as to leve on the buro when

he went to take his bath, witch no-body could account for disappearing, lest the rats carried it of, witch was a very serius loss. It cost 20 dollars, besides being so unbecoming to go balled in colled weather. So they said I must be a kleptomaniact.

But I'd like to kno what little boy with a pin an' a string could stand at a stove-pipe hole without going a fishing when the coste was clear! I was going to put the things back when I got a good chance; but they say kleptomaniacts offen return things, witch makes it planer I must be one. So now the hole is plastered up, and things is stupid genraly.

Every Fridy the profesur puts on a clene colar, an peple comes from the villedge in the afternoon to the xercises. Some boys read compo-sishuns, some recite peaces they have comited to memry, others have dialogs.

Miss Haven she brushes my hair that day, an' gives me a kiss, and tells me I look rele nice in my best suit.

" Now be a good boy, Georgie, so I will be proud of you."

I like her as well as I do my sis-ters, xcept Lil. I hope her ship will come in soon. I am going to visit her when it does. I wonder will she live on the ship. I hope so. I had to speke a peace to-day. I went up on a platform and made a bow, and spoke it very loud. Mrs. Pitkins rote it for me. The subjec was " School." She rote:

" How happy are our school days! The happiest of our lives!

" Little boys whose parents can

afford them the advantidges of a good scool should be very grateful to Provdunce. The poor children of the stretes long for such opportunities without avale. It is our duty to make the most of them while our minds are yung and plastic.

"Our nashun owes its grandyur to its facilitis of its educashun, among witch the bording-scool for boys, preparing for their collig, stands preemnunt."

That's what Mrs. Pitkins rote. I have it here to coppy in my diry. I cannot tell a lie. So I rote it over the way I wanted it myself, an' read an' read it very loud an' fast. She did not kno I had oltered it:

"Scool. Scool is horrid. Little boys whose fokes send them to scool are to be pitted. The poor children of the streets have a gollier time. They play from morning till nite hop-scotch an' marbles. I long to be a strete boy.

"Bording-scools is the worst kind. You can't have butter or pursurves but once; thare is more otemole than anything else. You have to stand on your head in the corner at the leste thing rong. If I was grone up, an' kept one, I would not be so cross as Mrs. Pitkins. This is all I know about scools."

I guess the peple thought it good for a boy of my size. They all smiled; the professur and Mrs. Pitkins smiled 2, as if it hurt them. When they had gone away an' I was strapping on my skates, to have sume fun the rest of the afternoon, Mrs. Pitkins come to me very sweet, an' says:

"You nede not trubble to put on your skates, Master Hackett; you will spend the remainder of the day in the scool-room, doing sums. What for did you olter what I rote, you wicked child! You must be nacherly depraved. If your father paid for 2 boys, it would be no rekumpense for the wurry of having such a bad boy, corrupting the other pupils."

She led me to the school-room, shut me in, and locked the door. It was cruel. I had looked forwurd all the week to Fridy. I could hear the other felloes shouting an' having lots of fun. The fire was out. I was that homesick it seemed to me Id fly into 10 thousan peaces. Evry sum I tride to do, the tears fell on the slate, that I didn't have to dip my sponge in water. My fingers were that numb I opened the stove door to see if the fire was burning yet; thare was just one cole. I tore up a copybook, and put the ruler on top of that; it blazed butiful; so I put on a lot of rithmeticks, till I got quite warm. But when I went to fix the stove-pipe, the old rikty thing tumbled down. I could not put it up agane; the smoke was fearful. I cride and cride, it smarted so; then I began to choke. I pounded on the door, and hollerd to Mrs. Pitkins to let me out. But she had gone to town with the key in her pocket. Miss Haven she told me to open the window an' lene my head out till she could get a man to open the dore. But the ice had stuck the windows tite; they would not budge. Miss Haven she was offul scart outside. She called to me:

"Brake the glass, Georgie, fore you sufocate."

I britened up when I heard her say that. In ten minutes there was not 1 hole pain of glass in those five windows. A man came and bursted in the door. The professur was pale with rath when he vued the ruin.

"What for did you brake the hull lot for, you little fool?" he asked me. "It will take a week to get this room in order. I shall send the bill to your father, sir."

"Adonijab," said Mrs. Pitkins, solemnly, "don't you think we had better send the boy along with the bill? We shall be ruined if we kepe him to the end of the term. He's wors'n the plages of Egip. I wish I had let him go skating; maybe he would have fell in an' drownded his-self."

Nobuddy seems to want me. My fokes sent me here coz they did not want me; and now Mrs. Pitkins wishes I was dead. I've made up my mind what I'm going to do. I saw something in a paper once : "Wanted, to adopt, a healthy male child." I'm going to send a letter to the paper for somebuddy to adopt me. I will say I am healthy. They will not dreme how bad I am. They will take me for a good little boy; such a sell on them! I'll rite it tonight. Jack Bunce will get it put in the paper for me. "A healthy male child wants to be adopted ; a good home more than wages."

CHAPTER XVI.

HE IS SUSPENDED.

THERE was quite a sceen last nite when I got home. I was put in the care of the conductor — the professur's last words were, "Conductor, kepe a sharp eye on that yungster ; he's a dredful hard case. I had to xpell him from my Academy ;" so when he come to punch my ticket he sorter laffed.

"What did you do to get xpelled, little chap?" he asked me. "You look as incent as a lamb," he added. 'I should not gess you were such a wicket felloe," and he patted me on the back.

"I did a hole lot of dredful things, sir," I ansered him. "I was a grate xpense to the profesur in wigs, but it was always a acksident—I never did things a purpus, never—it was gust my luck—I am very unlucky, sir," I added, with a depe si. "It was the last acksident I did that broke the camel's back—that's Mrs. Pitkins."

"Well," said he, "when I've been

through the trane I'll come back an you can tell me how it was."

So he came back an sat down in tother half the sete.

"Should you think, sir," said I, "they would xpell a little boy—a reel, nice, good little boy—gust for hooking a small peace of raw pi-crust out of the cook's pantry?"

"Well, no," said he, kind of thotful.

"They did," said I. "Oll I did in the world was to take a peace bout as big as my 2 fists—it wouldn't make more'n 1 dride appul pi Mrs. Pitkins thinks is helthy for children. I carrid it up to my room, cos the profesur was going to leckture on phisolgy down in the villidge that evening for the caws of the hethen, Mrs. Pitkins would be alone, so I woched my opportunty when she was in the kichen telling cook not to waste eg in the codfish for brekfnst, I put the pi-crust all over my face like I was a pi, and jabbed a hole, like cook does, where my mouth was; then I slipped into Mrs. Pitkins' room an got up on a chare in the corner with a shete rapped around me, coming down to the flore; it was dark in there, so she came in with a lamp in her hand, witch shone direckly on the gost—she gave a shreek an run. All would have gone well an no harm done, only the silly woman let go the lamp, which made a grease-spot on the carpet and set her dress on fire. She would have been burnd, only Jack Bunce put his overcote around her in the hall, so she gust got a blister on her hand, but her dress was spoilt—it was a

new one—and the frite brot on histericks offul, which she says she sees planely why my mother sent me off to school, but she wouldn't kepe me knot for 10,000 dollars in gold. I was sorry about her dress, so I gave her my five dollar gold-poace to by her another. She refused it. She said the dress would be put down in the bill. O dere, dere! what will papa say when he sees the bill? I've had so many acksidents! I'm olways in hot woter!

"Mr. Condukter, don't you nede a boy about my size to sell papers on the trane, or ham-sandwiches, or prize candy? I'd like to be abul to sport myself, I've cost so much for damages."

He sade that job was sold to a bigger boy.

"An now, my little chap," says he, "you remane quietly in your sete. Here's a ilstrated paper to look at. By and by I will see how you are getting along agane."

I thanked him very polite. So, gust as he went in the next car, the boy came along with prize candy. I bought 4 pakkages, and give him a dollar. I had been thinking I would try the bizness. As soon as he was out of site I gumped and went down the isle calling out "prize candy," like he did. Fokes smiled, but nobody buyed; so I opened the door an stepped out on the platform to try the next car.

It was offul windy, an I guess the cars joggled too mutch, for the next thing I knew I was skrambling out of a snow-bank. My ears were full of snow, so was my mouth—you never see! There was the trane most out of sight, cutting along like a thousand of brick, an I oll alone out in a field.

Miss Haven she cride when I went away from scool, an give me a peace of cake to eat on the way; it was in my pokkit, so I ate it then. It tasted offul good. So I had one pakkage prize candy left I was still holding onto; I thought I would eat that, then if I had to starve to deth, it would not be so hard, when I was cirprised to see the trane a coming along backwards like a crab. It made me laff; an there was the condukter, an oll the brakesmen, an the engineer, an fireman, oll leaning over looking for the peaces, and the windoes open, with the passengers' heds stuck out. But 200 peple got out when the trane stooped.

The condukter was pale as a gost, but when he saw me eting prize candy he flue into a fereful pashun.

"Get aboard!" said he. "I've lost 10 minnits! Get a bord, you little imp! What for did you play us such a trick?"

"I'm offul sorry, sir," said I; "I wont do it agane if I can help it. I didn't mene to; it was not me, it was the car—it joggled so."

He husseled me on bord, where I had a screus time with the ladies a crying over me and a feleing of my lims to see if I was broke. I had to give up all thoughts of the prize bizness for the present, but I am resolved to do somethin to sport myself if I mete with any more acksidents.

You see, dere diry, I didn't dare tell the conduktor what I reely was xpelled for, coz he mite bleve I did it on purpose. No boy but a very, very bad boy would purposely send a impurtnent Valentine to a lady like Mrs. Pitkins. The one I rote to Miss Haven had 2 duvs on it, an said:

"I shall try to improve and become oll that you wish, from your loving little friend, Georgie."

Mrs. Pitkins got one, which said:

"The rose is red,
The violets blue,
Pickles are sour,
And so are you."

Maybe Jack sent it, but she said the riting was mine. She didn't care about the valentine; that was nothing. What she made a fuss about was this: Some boy had put a peace of mete on a large fishhook, and fed her maltease cat, witch she wouldn't a cared so much about, only he had gone fishing in her glass globe, and cot all her goldfish, witch she could have stood if he hadn't gone skating Sunday afternoon, an' skated into an airhole, so that he was brethless when they got him out, and made such a mess with his wet close, she said her nerves were getting in a sad condishun. She was worn out. She really couldn't stand it—speshally when the very next day he blakked his face and hands with ink, got the kitchen broom, an tride to go up the sitting-room chimbly, an fell down an bumped his head a buiup as big as a goose eg, witch she would have forgot and forgivn if he hadn't pinned a peace of paper on her back, on witch was wrote: "This is the camel's back the last straw broke."

But that was only fun, and she wouldn't have minded it if she had not noticed that he had cut all the queer birds out of the dicshunnary, and made a long row of them on the wall behind his bed, so he would have something to amuse him when he waked up urly, witch made him brake the profesur's gold-bowed specktikels, putting them on the owl in the library, so they tumbled off; besides getting a friteful habit of coffing zactly like the profesur—only when he was sent to her room to study his geografy better, he got her nite-cap and nite-gown, an put them on Towser, making him howl so he run away and draged them all around the villedge.

So, when the conduckter came round agane, he had got over being mad about the trane losing time. My! Didn't the old thing fly! But I thot best not to menshun the above, so he said:

"Little chap, it's mity lucky you fell in a snow-bank. You couldn't do that twice. I gess you were born to .e hanged."

So I told him about the time I ran away in the frate car, an the brake-man was so kind.

"If they are cross at home cos I've come back, I'm going to let you know, Mr. Conduckter," said I. "I will live with you."

"You will have a tite time," said he; "I'm an old bachelor."

"So much the better," said I; "your wife won't be around to bother us. My sisters are real nice, bright, stylish girls, but they don't make allowance for boys. They won't let me play ball in the parlour when it's raining, or amuse myself like I ought to. They would like to stick me down in a wax chare, so I couldn't get up. Say, Mr. Conduckter, did your girl give you the mitten, the reason you're an old bachelor?"

He side an looked sad. Pretty soon he britened up and asked me would my sisters be down to the deppo to mete me. I didn't kno, so I didn't anser him.

"I would like a glimpse of them," he said. "You are most there, little chap."

Something got into my throte like it was a bone. I looked egerly out, when I saw the sign over Peter's grosery, an' the switchman with the wooden leg, an' the deppo, I would have cride if I had not winked. the teres back hard. Mr. Conduckter stood by the steps to see me safe off, and there was Sue looking offal sweet in a stunning hat and sele-skin cloke, an' Bess gust perfectly lovly, ready to hug an' kiss me, crying out:

"O, Georgie, you notty, bad, dere, deliteful boy, let me get at you!"

So I said:

"Mr. Conduckter, these are my sisters, but they are both engaged. I'm sorry for you; good-by; call an' see us. I'm much obliged. Ain't my sisters jolly?" an' he touched his cap an' laffed, an' the engineer, an' brakesman, an' everybody they cride "Hurrah! good-bye, little Georgie!" witch was very polite of 'm all.

Betty was down to the deppo, to, laffing an' crying like a goos:

"We've missed you dredful, Master Georgie; it's bin fereful quite with no Bad Boy to kepe us bissy."

"Indede it has," added Sue; " e've killed the fatted caf for our returned prodigy—it's all cooked an' on the tabel waitin','"—but it was not veal, after all, but roste turky with curent gelly, fride oysters, cold ham, floting iland, cake, presurves—suc a sprede. I et as if I had had no.hing but dry apple pi since I left home; only papa looked sollumly over the profesur's bill, an' manma turned very pale when I was telling the doctor how I got llowed offen the trane. Doctor Moore was very glad to see me, to; so was my squirl, he takes tea to our house offen, 'cause he an' Sue are going to get married in the spring.

After supper papa said:

"Georgie, I want you to turn over a new leef; you're getting older every day; try not to make so many mistakes; think *twice,* before you act *once*"—so the door was going to shut on the dog's tail, an' he said,

"Catch it, Georgie," but I waited to think twice which was death on the dog's tail.

The docktor says when I grow up I shall study medicine in his offis. His wallet what he kepes his medicine in was in his overcote pokkit in the hall, an' I thot it was a good chance to begin to be a doctor, so I took some white powder out of a little vial an' give a tiny bit to my squirl. I buried him this afternoon —Johnny came to the funeral.

O, how nete and pleasant my own room looks! How sweet my dremes last night! Betty is fatter than ever —she is a most obliging girl. My hart is full. I mene to try never, never to do rong agane so long as I live and brethe, so good-nite, my diry.

N.B.—Johnny an' I took Sue's work-box, the doctor give her Christmas, to bury my squirl in. I xpect Sue will not like it, but poor Bunny had to have a coughin. It made a lovly coughin.

CHAPTER XVII.

" GOODNESS ME! IT WAS THE CAT."

Dr. Moore and Sue have broke oph their engagement. It is a offul loss to Sue, coz she had her trooso all reddy. I'm afrade it will go out of stile before she gets another chance as good as the doctor, which is a first-rate feller, I think, and the stiles being so vaseline.

The wedding cake is not a dead loss so long as Johnny and I know the closet where it is kep; it is elegant cake, very useful when a boy is going skating or expecs not to get home in time for supper.

Last week there was a paragraf in the paper aganc; it made Sue cry till her eyes were as red as Johnny's were when I put red pepper in his mother's stove. I suppose black pepper would not make his eyes red. The paragraf ran thusly:

" Grate excitement prevales in fashnubble cirkles on ackount of a rumor that a certin marridge in high life is not to come oph after all. To our positive nollege the wedding cards have been engraved an were almost out; but the parties do not speke to each other now. The cause of this sudden change in the program is not made public— but it is whispered that it is *not* the gentleman's fault."

Poor Sue, I pity thee! How glad I am she does not gess it was her little brother put it in the paper.

Alas, how sad it is to carry round, day by day, a guilty conshune Alas, I am the cause why that engagement is broke off. All would be peaceful an sorene had Sue no bad boy for a brother. And yet I think that man they call Edison is more to blame than innocent little Georgie. What for did he go an take so much trubble to invent the electrick light? You see they were all talking about it, an how much money Mr. Edison would make, an what a fine thing it was, and the doctor he said he had a battery in his back offis, which I knew was grate fun, coz he let me take hold one of the handles oncst—so in the morning I told Johnny, an he an me watched till the doctor went oph in his buggy, an then we climbed into the window of his back offis, and I pored some stuff into it out of a bottle like I had seen him do, an I give Johnny the handles to hold, an he just hopped rite oph the floor, an then he fell down and stretched out. I hollered to him to let go the handles, but he didn't say a single word, like he was dead, so I got the handles away from him an told him to sit up, which he didn't pay any attention, an I was fritened, coz I am very fond of Johnny, so I went an got some men, who had to climb in the window, too. They threw cold water on him, and said I was a naughty boy—they guessed I'd killed him, so they carried him home, an Johnny's mother she wont speke to me now. I think she ought to be thankful her child came 2, which he did after a long, long time. So Doctor Moore he scolded me perfeckly offul. He said I was ruining his practice—that folks were afrade to take his medsin for fear I had had a finger in it—that I was a nice little boy as he ever seen when I behaved myself, but I musn't touch his things. 1 told him I was offul sorry—would never do it agane. I ment to keep my prommis fatheful, so the next time I was in there long with him I seen a mouse running in and out a hole in the floor. I thought I would do him a favor, seeing I had been such a nusance : so that night, about dark, as he was going home to tea, I put our cat in the offis to catch the mouse quick, so the doctor wouldn't see her. He came to visit Sue after supper, and I should infer he stade rather late. When he got back to his offis, where he sleeps in the back room, he herd the fere-fullest catterwauling like a thousand cats was having a serious time which made him unlock the door an go in an strike a light as soon as possible. Poor Pussy! the mouse have got on the shelf, and she gumped after it, for all the bottles was knocked off an broken all to smash ; you never see such work, the nasty medsin on his nice, new carpet, but kitty fared the worst. A bottle of vitrol got broke, and she put her foot

in it ; no wonder she mewed and spit like she was crazy, so when the doctor went in she flew rite at his face, but he put his arm up luckily— that saved him his eyes—so she only scratched his nose and forrid—that made him look ridickelous next day —and when he knocked her oph at last, she made a beeline for the door, and nobody has seen her since. The horrid oil of vitrol, it et a large hole in the carpet, which would not have been quite so bad, only it hit the lounge before it rolled off on the floor, and scattered lots of the horrid stuff all over his new suit, which came home that day, which he was to be married in. It was utterly spoiled.

I don't think the affare would a been quite so serious, bad as it was, only when he came to our house the next morning to relate the axdent, Sue she burst out laughing when she saw his face all courtplaster, his nose twice its naturel size, an she laughed and laughed, like she could not stop, so he said :

"It may be fun for you, Miss Hackett, but its deth to me. I've had enuff of that little brother of yours, and of you, too, if this is all the thanks I get for what I've had to put up with. I don't beleve I can stand marrying into the family of a boy like George. So, good-bye, for-ever, Miss Susan," an he slammed the door real hard, and walked away as stiff as if he was froze.

So then Sue she began to laugh out of the other side of her mouth, but it was all up—he hasn't been near her sence, an that's two weeks ago ; so I sent an account, on the sly, to the paper, which is certain to be put in.

The hull family is down on me about the cat, which I did from the best of motives. Who could have fourseen that Sue would dye an ole made gust because I put a cat in her telloe's offis to catch a mouse? It is my luck. I am a most unlucky boy. Sue, she won't eat enough to kepe a bird alive, an' Bess boxes my ears every time she gets close enuff, as if boxing a little boy's ears was going to make the doctor come back enny sooner. Sue says she could forgive him every thing except his putting that paragraf in the papers—" it was not the gentleman's fault." Well, was it? So I said so; but I hope an' pray she won't discover who did it. I've done enough mischief without being found out; that would cap the climax.

Yesterday Sue had another crying spell; the girls were in their room, where I was hid in their closet cutting up one o' their rubber shoes in strips to make a ball, an I heard Bess a telling her doctor Moore was said to be going evvry nite to see Agness Jewell. Juge Jewell is a big bug, an Agnes is said to be the mos stilish girl in town now. Our Lil is married and gone away; so Sue she was that gellus she cried herself into fits, and would not go down to supper, which made it offul inconvenyant for me to get out of that there closet. I thought I should starve to death, but when it got very dark I slipped out as stiff as a mouse; so when she didn't find her rubber, Bess always said a rat must have carried it oph to sleep in.

When I was eting my supper alone, except Betty who brought me a peice of pie, which she didn't want for dinner, I made up my mind I was too retched to eat anything but the pie an some cake, with Sue up stairs comiting suicide by slo starvation, an if I could make amends for the mischuff I had done I would do it. I said to Betty:

" Tell the folks not to worry bout me—I'm going to call on a frend; I'll be back in half an hour."

With that I slid out of the back door. Bout 10 minutes later I was ringing at Juge Jewell's door.

" Is Miss Agnes in?" I asked her. She said she was; I said I wished to see her a moment. She said :

" Step right into the parlor."

I took oph my cap, and stepped.

Miss Agnes was at the piano, dressed to kill, her hair banged, her cheeks red. She began to laugh when she seen me.

" How do you do, Master George?" said she.

Said I :

" Miss Agnes, did you ever hear Pinafore ?"

" Lots of times," said she.

Said I :

" Do you remember that exciting part of it where it says:

"'Goodness me! that was the cat?'

That's gust the way it was at the doctor's office; it was the cat. An now, Miss Agnes, do you think it is onest and right for him to brake my sister's heart because the cat nocked oph a few of his nasty medsin bottles? I want you to tell him from little Georgie when he comes here to-night, that Sue don't come to her meals half the time, she has lost her appetite, her dresses are getting too big for her; the reason she laughed when she saw his nose, was because she had the histeriks, she was so alarmed, and folks who have the histeriks have to laugh no matter how much they don't want to. It is a shame the way he treated her, an little Georgie is going to sue him for breach of prommis, gust as true as I live, an breathe, an draw the breath of life; an' when I grow up I am going to fight a duel, he can't escape."

Gust then somebody behind me put their hand over my mouth, an then they lifted me oph my feet an put me on their shoulder, an I looked down, and there it was the doctor himself! Did you ever!

"No, Georgie," says he, "we won't fight any duels, we will make up an be friends once more. I feel gust as bad as your sister does. I gess the best thing I can do is to go home with you an' tell her so, if Miss Jewell will excuse me." So, e went.

When we got there, I said:

"Go in the parlor, doctor, I'll go up stairs an call her down; she is crying her eyes out up thare in the dark. The folks are in the sitting-room."

Then I ran up stairs, bounced in her room, and hollered out:

"Where are you, Sis? You are wanted down stairs. There's a show in the front parlor, the grate 'What is it?' has got away from Barnum's."

She grabbed my arm so tight it is black and blue.

"What do you mean, Georgie?" says she, catching her breth.

"I mean t'other girl's cake is dough."

With that she flew down stairs like the wind. I follered as fast as I could, but I didn't get there as soon as I would like, cause I stopped to wind the clock in the hall, which broke cause it was winded the day before, and now it'll have to be mended, I spose: but when I did get down there was a tablo in that parlor—let the curtain fall. Little Georgie is in high favor gust at present. They didn't even grumble when they found what a offal hole some mouse had made in the wedding-cake. "We can make another," Sue said, quite careless like. The ceremony is to come oph as soon as the plaster does from the doctor's nose.

CHAPTER XVIII.

HE MAKES AND FLIES A KITE.

Rosa Prince is going to give a party; she is quite a big girl; the party will be her tenth birthday. She says they are going to have a splendid time, somebody to play the piano to dance by, a real supper on a long table, not passed around; but she don't know as she can invite me, because I am rather young and very bad; her mother said she had better leve me out. I told her she was mistaken, I was getting to be a model boy, she mite ask my mother was I not offul good these days; it was mean to leve me out; if she did I would leve her out when I gave my phansey party, which mama says I may sometime, if I continue good. So she asked me, and I am going. It is to-morro night.

I am going to our village school now; I hope to improve in my spelling and writing very fast, the teacher says I am brite enuff to run for President, if I would only pay attenshun; but there are a hundred things in school to distract a boy's attenshun, more than one would think who had never been there. There are no flies in winter, but there are spitballs enuff to make up, and looking around on the sly, to see what boy is making signs to you, takes up a great deal of time, as also drawing the teacher on your slate, with a cold in his head, which you rub out after you have held it up; also eating a napple against the rules behind the lid of your desk, an setting his teeth on edge with your slate-pencil, which *will* scratch. I have very little time for study; but it is better than being sent to boarding-school. Bess says the house is like a paradise when I'm in school; I asked her were there angels in paradise, cos I did not see none there. I'm tezing her to make me a kite; she says she has no time until the wedding is over; all the boys have them; it is coming kite-season; it is stupid to loaf around and see the other boys fly theirs. I gess I'll go to the shop and buy two sticks, and make a kite myself; I can make it up in my room; Betty will clear up the muss; I'll get papa's bottle of mucilage, mamma's scissors, a few newspapers, and the string-bag; I'll get it done before I go to school in the morning.

* * * This is the night of Rosa Prince's party; I feel very lonesom, sitting in my room with the door locked on the other side; I spose they are having a jolly time with their fine supper; I aint had none—not a thing to eat since my lunch, which I et at eleven; I am very hollow inside like a drum. But what do these heartless parents of mine care how their child suffers? *They* are groan up—their trials are over—nobody shuts them up and locks their door an tells them they can have no supper, when they are sick, an misrable, an hungry; noboddy cuffs their ears when they did not kno any better; noboddy makes them study spelling and grammar when they want to go and have some fun; they don't have to sit down in a chare an never open their mouth when company comes, and they are just bursting with all the news they have to tell.

I made my kite this morning like I said I would. I got up very early and crep down in my stockings to get the stuff so as not to wake the folks. I did not get any sticks at the carpenter's, for I looked at papa's silk umbrella an made up my mind the whalebones in that would answer the ticket; so I got it down in the hall an took out what bones I wanted, and then I cut up the silk to make the tail—I made that first—a golly long one. Then I cut out my kite and pasted it; by the time breakfast was ready it was done, so I hid it under the bed until it was time to go to school.

I was axdently very late to school that morning—in fact I did not get there until school left out in the afternoon, an the teacher had gone home. You see it took so long to fly my kite I had no time to arrive thare before; the string was a mile long, which nacherly took a good while to let it all out an take it all in again, which was what made me late. So the teacher he stopped and asked our folks if little Georgie was sick, cause he didn't come to-day, an that gust .et the cat out of the bag.

So when I got to school the boys were flying their kites, and I flew mine again; there was a stiff breeze an they went up butiful, but mine came down on a horse's head on Mane street what was afraid of everything, even a kite, an he ran away like blazes, and threw the man out on top of his head against a hiching-post which was too bad for it broke the post like anything; I'm afrade they will have to put up a new post. The man is killed, they say, though some think he will come to his senses again. If he does I hope he will kno better than to drive a scary horse; it is always dangerous.

The man said I must not fly my kite on Mane street any more; so I went oph down by the depo cause I knew the engines want afrade of kites, an I let her fly. Good gracious you ought to seen her go. Little Johnny sade it went gust like a bird; I let him hold the string awhile; we had an offul lot of fun, only when she settled down she got cot in the top of a big tree on Jefferson strete, an we could not get her out; we tride and tride, so I had ten cents the doctor gave me last night, an I told Johnny if he would go up in the tree an bring her down I would give him the ten cents. I did not like to go because my ma had told me never to climb high trees—I mite fall out.

Johnny said he was afrade; I said: "Nonsense, Johnny; I did not know you was a cowrd; you can buy a lot of taffy with ten cents."

Then he went up, but he had only got about half way up when he lost his hold or a limb broke, an he fell down; so I had to leve my kite up there, which was awful mean, the first day I made it. It hurt little Johnny some, falling out of the tree; his leg is broke; he will have to lay in bed six weeks. Doctor Moore has mended it, and put it into sticks 'or sumthing. Poor Johnny, I want to see him dredful, to ask him how it feels, but his mamma won't let me go near him; Betty says she says when Johnny gets well they are going to move away—she will not risk his life any longer in the naborhood of such a wicked, wicked boy. She is real mean; I love him an I wouldn't hurt him for anything. I did not kno he would fall: if he had held on like I told fore he went up perhaps he would not broke his leg, an I gave him the ten cents. I do wish I could see how funny he looks with it done up in sticks. Betty says mamma feels so bad she's gone to bed sick; what for is she going to bed? It was not her leg that was broke. Some folks is so foolish you don't kno what to think of em.

And Betty says papa is friteful rathy about his best umbrella; they found the pieces in my room, so they knew I cut it up; when I come home he took me by the shoulder and pushed me up stairs into my room, an locked the door; nobuddy, not even Betty, has brot me some supper; I do wish families would not have bad boys to make mistakes an then have to go hungry, after playing hard all day an getting such a dredful sinking to their stummick. If I could get a messidge to Mr. Bergh, I'd send him word how I was treated. Johnny

was too small to be invited to the party, so he need not make such a fuss cause his leg is broke. He will have gelly, an chicken-broth, an lots of good things. O, my, how hungry I am: I wish I was in his place. I wish I was to Rosa Price's party cting ice-creme. I wish I was in Robinson Cruso's hut cting fride clams. I wish I had a bread-fruit tree a growing in this room. If I had a lamp I could read bout such things in my books, but no, even this dere diry, I have to scrall by moon-lite on the window-sill—all consulation is denide me. I guess I'll go to bed an try an dreme about the ship-recked sailors that was took on board, an was fed an kindly treated—better than poor Georgie is.

*   *   *   *

Mamma let me out of my room after papa went to business, this morning. She talked to me a long time with tears in her eyes, how sorry she was I was so full of mischief, an poor Johnny's leg was broke, an I cride like everything, an promised I'd try to kepe out of scrapes, and I asked her what did they have for breakfast, and did Johnny's leg look funny? So she gave me some gridle-cakes an maple-syrup, and said Johnny's mother would never, never let me speak to Johnny again. I'd get him into hot water so oftun, wich is a offul falsehood. Whatever I have done, I never got Johnny in hot water, did I? I want to see him so bad I feel as if I couldn't wait. I have never seen a broken leg, and I have something serious on my mind —I want him to give me back my ten cents, cause he did not get my kite. Good-by, dere diry, I am oph for school. When school is out I'll try an get my kite.

I could not get it, an so I'm going to make anuther, like that picture in the boy's book of the turtle kite. It will be first rate. When I come home this afternoon I was out in the back yard, tying the tails of my two kittens together an hangin them on the close-line to dry, coz I'd made them get wet falling in the cistern, when I saw Johnny's mother going oph down street with a bottle in her hand like she was going to get some medicine. Says I :

"Now's my time to see my poor little friend—his mother's out—I know Johnny is asking to see me."

I climbed up on their woodshed, over their kitchen roof, an went in the window upstairs in the hall, and crep softly to Johnny's room. When I got thare he was lying quiet—nobudy in the room. I said :

"How are you, little chap? How pale you are. Duz your leg hurt very bad? I wish I could see it —I never saw a broken leg—it must look queer. Oh, my, what a lot of gelly! Johnny, let me look at your leg, that's a good little boy, I won't hurt it a mite—I gust want to see how it looks."

Then I tasted of his current gelly, took a drink of his tea, an gust softly lifted the sheet. I couldn't see his leg one bit, it was all done

up in funny sticks and bandiged— I had to take them all oph before I could see it. Johnny cried and said I musn't tutch it, but I told him I would be offul careful—didn't he want to see where it was broke, too ? So he let me.

There was not much to see after all—I had my trubble for my panes —gust a swelled place—I thought it would be in 2 pieces.

"'Taint even bent," said I, disgusted ; then I moved it up and down to see would it go, but he hollered and scremed that fereful I was fritened, an the way I got out at that window over them roofs was a caushun!

I don't kno what Dr. Moore ment telling papa this evening I was a cruel, barberis boy. I may axidently happen to be a bad boy now an then, but I am not a barberis boy—Joe Punk is one—and papa groned like he had the toothake an said he bet he would have to move out West on a hundred mile farm to kepe me away from the nabors. The doctor said Johnny's leg had to be set over agane, witch hurt worse than at first.

Poor, poor little fello ! I'd be a frend to thee if they would let me, but they wont—his mother's got a loaded pistol, an she's thretened to shoot me if I go near him. I am warned to keep out of danger. I am glad my mother is not that sort of a woman like poor little Johnny's.

CHAPTER XIX.

HE ENJOYS THE FIRST OF APRIL.

I DID not sleep at home last night or night before, cos I made a unxpected visit to dear Lil, so I could not write in thee, my diry. You see, dear diry, day before yesterday was the furst day of April. They call it April Fool Day. The boys were telling for days wot they were going to do, but I kept quiet, like an owl, which papa says keeps up an offal thinking.

It has been offal dull since Johnny broke his leg, cos his mother don't allow me to go there—she kepes a pistol loaded, so they say—an I was aking to have some fun. Everybody says the town is fritefull dull when little Georgie Hackett ain't in mischief; they wish his sister wood get married an done with it, and so she will next week if nuthing happens; but to go back to the furst of April.

They have got a new town-hall bilt since the other one was burnt by some silly girls screming at a mouse with a very large bell, which rings very fast when there is a fire. Well, the nite before I ate a harty supper, an lade in a supply of wedding-cake; my plans were lade to get lost under a bench while the temprunce leckture was getting preched by a lo-looking felloe, who said he knew how it was himself. I hired anuther boy with my Jack-knife an some cake to get lost too; we had a lot of fun after the ganitor put out the lights and locked the dore.

I've herd my mamma sat up all night, witch was foolish of her : she might have knone I was all right. We wated and wated till we fell asleep, and then I woke up an wispered :

" Willie, it is time—its most dalite. Come on."

We groped our way to the big rope behind the stairs, an gerked an gerked gust as fast as we could, as if the hull town was on fire.

Everybody sprung out of bed an put on their close in a dredful hurry. We could hear em run an holler, " Where is it ? Do you see it ?" O, it was fun ! In 10 minits the streets was like a prosession. So as soon as he could get his boots on an come, the ganitor unlocked the door and flue in like mad. It was getting quite light, so he could see us, an he stoped an opened his mouth like we were oysters.

I asked him did he kno wot day it was, an he got that mad he shook me till my head felt like a rattle box; but yung Mr. Spriggs, the lawyer, he laffed, an said :

" Let the boys be. Own up you're fooled, old felloe, along with the rest of us. Bully for you, boys—you've got the hull town. I'll trete, for one!

So the folks went home, an took more time to make their toylets, speshally Miss Hanks, who unforchunitly forgot her teeth, an Mr. Sponce, who didn't have time to take his hair out of curl papers.

I walked home with papa who did not scold a bit, so at brekfast Sue said, " Georgie, you must be hungry getting up so urly, here's some fritters," an Betty put a hull dish full in frunt of me. I'm very fond of nice hot fritters for brekfast so I piched in. " Wot nasty tuff ole fritters," said I after a while an the family laffed like enny thing—they were cotting batting fritters diped in egg an fride, and they would not give me a single thing to ete but them.

I had red in the papers about the pokket book trick. I thought it would be fun to try it—drop an ole pokket book an wotch to see who will pick it up; so when I went up to brush my hair for school, I sliped in mamma's room an took her wallet out of the buro drawer. There was only one bill in it so I stuffed it out nice an round with brown paper, an started urly, so as to have some sport before school began. I put it down on the pavement an hid behind a dry-goods box for I saw a horrid ole tramp coming, of course he lited on the wallet and crammed it in his pokket an walked away, that fast he didn't limp like he was lame any more. " Oho, ole scamp," says I, "wont you be mad when you open it !" So I stroled along easy to the telegraf offis which I knew the operator there, he is a frend of mine cos he's ded in love with Bess an I

borroed a envelope an shete of paper when he was not looking and pretty soon I went away, cos I was in a hurry to get Jim Blake, what rites a better hand than I do, to rite it, " Doctor Moore, come kwick. Lily is very sick—not expected to live. Montagu," witch I had a boy take to his offis gust in time for him to cotch the next train if he hurrid ; then I happened down to the station behind a irate-car when he came running to the train. Oh, how I laffed. It was an offul good goke. I knew the telegraph paper would make him think it was in ernest. By that time it was too late to go to school ; I mite as well make a day of it. I took my gold dollar an stuck it to the pavement with shoemaker's wax like I'd seen men do with pennies ; lots of folks burnt their fingers, but a big boy came along an he took his gnife an ripped it up an put his finger to his nose an carrid it away—disgusting. I call that no better than steling. Then I stroled on past the mildam an put my hed in Mrs. McKearny's cottidge, and asked her did she know little Benny had fell in the pond, which made her schreech like she was crazy and fall down on the flore—such a simpleton !—as if she could not remember it was April Fool.

I was friteful hungry by that time on akount of the cotton batting fritters, an I sat down on a log to ete my lunch wot Betty had put up for skool. There was a nice mince turnover of witch I am partikurarly fond. I took a large mouthful. It was composed of sawdust and black pepper

—nasty stuff. I knew who did it, it was Bess, so I thru it away an sawndered on till I came to the florists, who does not no me very well, because he has not lived here very long, an I went in.

I had the telegraf oprater's card witch I borrowed when I borrowed the paper, an I said to the florist:

"Put up your best and bigest bokay—bout five dollars worth, an tack this card on, and send it rite away to Miss Bess Hackett, an the bill to the telegraf offis."

So he did it.

When I came out Juge Jewell's daughter was going by; I ran after her an told her "Miss Agnes, here's yur nice lace hankerchif," but she went strate on, coz she remembered it was the 1 of April, so I put it in my pokket, which she had realy lost it. By this time I was desprit hungry an I went into Peter's grocery to buy a cent's wurth of peanuts, very filling at the price; I also bot some raisons, cheese, ginger cakes, crackers, an a pound of dates, witch was charged to our folks, an I sat on the counter an laffed at Peter's gokes an had a good time. He was taking it easy, telling the tricks he played wen he was a boy. All of a sudden he gumped as if he was hot.

"Wot's that?" he cride.

A dark, thick streme was floing all along the flore among the barels an' boxes everywhere.

"Praps your molases barel has sprung a leek," says I.

He gave me a sharp look, but I went on eating cheese; so he ran, an sure enuff some careless person had left it running. There was bout six galons of the sticky stuff over everything. I was dredful sorry—such a waste of syrup!

"I bet you did it, you little imp!" said Peters.

He made a grab, I dodged, he steped in the molases, sliped an fell. You never saw such a sight as he was when he got up. I did not remane very long to hear what he said; my mamma says to alwas come away when persons use bad languige, so I went.

After that things was sort of dull for awhile. I kept straing sloly along, looking out for something to amuse me, till I come to the new railroad cut, where the men were blasting rocks; but they were eting their dinner, cos it was noon, so I thot I would have some fun with a can of powder witch was left there. There was a new bridge—you never herd such a racket in all your life as it made when it blew up. I should certinly have been killed only I was in the tunnel. Such a dust! My! the air was full. You could hardly see the folks when they came running, witch was lucky for me, for I was offul fritened after it was done, and I hid all the afternoon till supper time.

It is very rong to tell falsehoods, I seldom do it. When I come in mamma sprung up and clasped me in her arms.

"I was afrade my darling was blue up," she gasped, "cos you had not been to school, nor could we find you. Georgie, there has been a terribul axdent—the new railroad bridge blue up this noon—did you hear the xplosion?"

I said I heard something like thunder bout that time.

"That was it," she said.

"How did it happen?" I inquired.

"It is a mystery—no one knows."

"Perhaps," said I, "them careless workmen did it with their cans of powder."

Papa came in an said he believed the thery was some dinamite had bursted.

"It was a grate pity," he added; "such a costly bridge."

So we all went to supper.

"It's so strange," said Sue, "the doctor has not been in once to-day. I don't understand it."

Bess had a bunch of lilys of the valley in her dress, a rose in her hair, she was fixed up, an looked as proud as a pecock.

"Where did you get so much flowers, Bess?" I asked her.

"O, somebuddy sent them!" she answers, coloring up red.

"By the way, Georgie darling," mamma said, "have you seen my wallet? I'm very anxious about it, for I cannot find it. There was a $100 bill in it, my bridal present to your sister. I'm afrade some sneke-thefe has stolen it."

A one $100 hundred dollar bill! I felt kind of fante, an drank a full goblet of cold water before I rallid enuff to reply :

"Dere mamma, I thot it was a 1 doliar bill; I hope that tramp will bring it back when he finds what's in it. I gust did it to April fool him."

The hull family looked blank—mamma groned. Sue said, O dear ! Gust then the bell rang an Betty brought papa a bill from the grosry for half a barel of molases witch Master George Hackett had turned the spigot, also a suit of close, a pound of dates, a ounce of cheese. While papa was reading it the doctor come in ; he looked very sober like he was tired an cross.

"Where have you been all day ?" asked Sue, gumping up an hugging him that tite about the neck I should think he would strangle.

"Ask that little angel sitting there!" says he.

"Georgie," cride Sue, "wot under the sun an moon have you been up to now after your sollum promise to behave ?"

"Theres only one coarse of tretment will cure him," said the doctor, offul serious, "with your permission, sir," to papa, "I'll try it on him after supper. I will give him a dose of pills, then I will bleed him, after that blister him all along the spine, an put a row of cups on his chest; then I will chloroform him an cut oph both his legs—that will stop his badness for awhile. Do you consent ?"

Papa said he did.

So I went out in the kitchen very sudden an borroed a dollar from Betty to pay my fare, an I cut stick for the depot where I got to Lil's at 10 that night. She had gust gone to bed, but she got up an fixed me comfortable on the sofa. O how she nffed when she told me how the doctor looked when he rushed in an found her sitting soing by the window; but she scolded too an made me promise never to do it again no matter if it was the 1 of April. She said, "practikle gokes was very foolish, wikked, injurious things;" so I thot I had better not menshun the bridge, I am reel sorry about that. I've added up the bill, an I don't think it pays.

Peter's bill, $25 dollars.
Bokay, $5 dollars.
Mamma's purse, $100 dollars.

Doctor's railrode fare, $2 dollars.
Mine ditto.
Railrode bridge, $30,000 dollars.

Still I don't think a little boys leg ought to be cut oph because he's fond of April Fooling. I got dere Lil to rite a note to the doctor begging him to xcuse me once more; he says he will gust this once.

N.B.—Bess was so mad she would not speke to me when I come home —why didn't that telegraf felloe pay the bill an kepe dark ?

CHAPTER XX.

THE WAY HE EARNED HIS PONY.

THERE isn't a sole about the house but me an Bess xcepting the help, for papa and mamma have gone to spend a week with Lil, and the doctor an his bride are at the hotel. Mamma said she did hope Georgie would keep out of mischief while they were away—she should fret about him all the time, but I ashured her she nede not wurry—I would be as good an quiet as the day was long, go to scool reglar, come home strait as soon as scool was out, mind my sister and behave generly. Papa said if I suckseded he would think about bying me that canadin pony that the bucher is bound he shall take for $ forty (40) dollars. I would ruther have a pony than 6 by-

sickles. I have dremed of that pony evry nite since the bucher told me about him—he is a little buty. I shall try my level best to be as good as pie. Betty says it is all in trying, it is esy to be a good boy a week if you only try, but I don't see how she knows for she never was a boy, but I will try. A live pony with a saddle an bridal thrown in is wurth stop stoning dogs and running away from scool for. Next week how proud I shall be riding down mane street to call on my sister Sue at the hotel. I must keep a fathful rekord of my good behavior.

Papa and mamma have been gone over one night. I was pretty good yesterday. I broke the looking-glass in mamma's room, but that was an axdent. Me an Charlie were playing ball in there with the door shut, so as not to disturb Bess. The ball bounced offul cause there was so much rubber in it after I had fixed it up with Bess' overshoes; it hit the glass an nocked over a colonc bottle which spilled on the new tidy, so we came out an played ball in the back yard.

Betty will be sprised next time she goes in there. It begun to sprinkle, so we come in an I told my sister me an him would go to the garret to play. It was luvly up there, only in some places there was no floor, an when I stepped on it to see if it would hold me the plaster all come down in the spare bed-room—too bad! plaster makes such a mess on a carpet and a silk quilt. I would not have stepped on it if I had knone it would not hold.

There was a nold trunk full of letters, so I gave Charlie about 100 to paste together to make a kite. We took the rest and bilt a fire in such a funny old stove that was cracked on the bottom so fire fell through, but we put it out; I had to run and get my bedroom picher and pore on, but we got it out, so I gess I will get my pony. There was not much harm done.

We came down to supper in grandpa's cloes, so Betty had to take them back before dark, witch was lucky, for the fire was not quite out. It was lively for all hands till we got it out.

Bess said I must go to bed urly like a good boy, so I went at 8.

Would you believe it, when I went down bout an hour after to get a drink of water out of the ice picher in the dining-room, I saw that telegraf oprator sitting on the sofa beside of Bess through the key-hole, an when I hollered "boo" very sudden, he gumped as if he thought there wus a trane coming in. Bess got up and opened the door, but I was not there, I was getting a drink in the dining-room, so she shut the door an sat over on the other side of the room.

My parents have been away 2 nights an days. I am still trying to be good. I told the bucher to-day to feed my pony up well, so he would be in good order—he said of course. Would I like to take a little ride to try him? I said I would. It made me fereful late to school, but I shall not tell Bess. I stopped to the telegraf offis, there was a big crowd there, coz it was time for the train ; I did not get oph the pony, I hollered hullo.

"Hullo yourself," said the oprator, through the little windo.

So I ast him what for my sister Bess gumped up oph the sofa an sat on the uther side of the room when I gust said "boo" through the key-hole.

He got as red as fire, coz the hull crowd laffed like they would go into fitz.

I played with the bucher's little boy a while when I got back with the pony. We played he was a caff, but I gess if his father had not come when he did the caff would have been strangled to death, he pulled so hard on the rope, but that was not my fault, it was the caff that pulled, oll I did was to hold the rope.

The bucher said I had better go to school, so I went. Bess said I must bring no more boys home with me, so I brought little Flora Adams. It was windy, an' we went out in the yard to fly my new kite. The doctor made it for me; it is very large, an has to have a very strong string, for it pulls like a horse when it gets up high an the wind is strong. I tell you it went up golly. I was offul frade I could not hold it alone, so I got Flora to help. I tied the end of the string round her waste and told her to brace herself agenst the wood-shed door. The cat came round the corner, so I told her to hold on for dear life while I put the cat over the fence to make Johnny's dog growl. Pritty soon, when the cat's tail had got about as big as my arm, an Towser was growling, I herd a friteful screme, an looking round, there was poor Flora going up like a streak, gust as if she were a foul of the air. I tride to grab her shoes, but was not quick enuff. That offul kite had been too much for her! I don't beleve she braced herself. I was very much surprised to see how easy it took her up. Before I could say Jack Robson, there she was rite over Mr. Shattuck's three-story brick house. She looked offul funny. I gess folks wondered what made her fly, for you could not see the string at all.

Ole Miss Pendleton told Bess afterwards she certainly thought the millenial had come. The hull town says that child had a provdenshal escape from a horribul death; but gust as she flew over Mr. Shattuck's house the string gave way, and she fell on the roof, witch was a flat one with a railing around, so they rushed up and got her; she wasn't one bit hurt, only scart, but I lost my splendid kite. I think her folks ought to give me another, cos if she had braced herself like I told her, she would not have lost my kite. Betty has discovered the hole in the scaling; I told her I thought the rats must have knawed through. It was stupid after Flora went home, with no kite, so I took a walk. It was warm and pleasant, though breezy — such wether as makes a boy feel like he'd like to go fishing. I bought some fish-hooks an a line into Peter's, and strade along until I came to the mill-dam where I most got drowned last spring. It was supper time, but I knew Betty would save me some, so I took it easy. I dug some angel worms, and caught a good many weeds, and most caught two minnows, only they got away, but about dark I caught a real live eel—a great big fellow, most as big as a alligator—so I took it home for breakfast, but I had some fun first. I took it in the parlor when no one was there, and curled it up on the peanno like a big black snake, and then I et my supper. Betty lited the lamps, an my sister come down stairs all fixed up as if she expected compny, an set down to the peanno, and begun to sing:

"For I'm little butter-cup—
Dear little butter —"

cow! Wough! Ee—e! Ough! Eeeee! you never hurd! A locomotive whissel would be ashamed of itself to sqoll like that. Of course I rushed in to see wot was up. Cook and Betty they run in to. Bess she flu by like she wos a eat in a fit rite into the middle of the strete.

"It is sunthing on the peanno, I gess," I said to the cook, so she went up, kind of slo like, and she took a look.

I was def as a post for over 2 hours the way those two silly cretures yelled. Sevrul nabors came in to know wot was the matter.

"A good eel," said I.

"Wot?" said they.

"A good eel," said I, and then I laffed. "I do beleve women are born nervous," I told them, "to make such a fuss about an eel they will eat without hollering a bit when it's on a platter."

They said I was a naughty boy to friten my poor sister so, praps she wouldn't get over it for a week. That's always the way—little Georgie is always to blame, even when his grone-up sister don't know an eel from a black snake! * * * My dear parents have been absunt 3 days an nights. I am getting along tolrabul well, though my sister is vexed about my going fishing agane all day yesterday in my best suit, witch I put on because it was Friday at scool an the teacher xpeeted visitors. If I had knone I would have stade away rom scool, I would have worn my uther clocs, for I tore my new ones badly, and got some tar on my jacket where I hit it agenst the wagon wheel when I was under the wagon taking out the pin so the wheel would come off an the flour barels would burst open and the flour would fly. I tell you it was golly fun. Three barels busted. I got a good eel of flour on me, playing in it after it broke, witch is hard on new clocs.

I did not catch many fish, there was so much els to do. I came home bout 4 an went in the back door, up to my room, an put on my old suit so Bess wouldn't scold.

Bess is a offul coward. She's that frade of burglars she can't sleep nights, now papa an mamma are away, so she keeps that telegraf oprator sitting up in the parlor till 12 or after. Then she goes up stares, looks all round, and under her bed, and leaves the lamp burning, an don't dare to take a nap. I don't see wot makes girls such cowards.

I tell you I was hungry when I went down to supper. My sister ide me sturnley.

"George," sade she, "the teacher has been here agane to report your absunce. Where have you been all day?"

"Fishing," was my reply.

"When do you expect to learn to write and spell propurly," she ast, "if you waste your time? Did you bring home anuther snake?"

I told her no; 1 was enuff.

"Georgie, I have asked in a few yung folks to spend the evening, I am so lonesum. Go and put on your new suit, behave like a little gentleman, an I will allow you to sit up till 10."

"What is it smells so?" she said,

sniffing, when I came in the parlor. " O, Georgie ! what have you got on your new jacket ?"

But her friends came, an she could say no more. I was so tired I kept very still an polite all the evening, only when Betty brought in the tray with cake and lemenade, I happened to put out my foot and she stumbled, an the lemenade went over everything. Betty is a very owkward servant. But I was sent to bed.

I gess I had been asleep about two hours when I was woke up by the offulest screming, like the house was on fire. I got up an peeked out in the hall. Bess came rushing in her night-gown, an pushed me in an turned the key.

" O, Georgie !" she panted, there's a horrid big burgler under my bed."

She threw up my window and called help, murder, fire, till some of the nabors came and gnocked on the door, an I had to go down an let them in. Bess an cook an Betty oll rushed down an threw theirselfs into the men's arms.

" Wot is it ?" ast the nabors.

"A man under my bed; I saw him gust as plain as day," gasped Bess.

" O, don't go up without your armed —he'll murder you !"

So 2 of them went up : 2 staid with Bess, coz she hung on so they could not help it. I follced them to my sister's room. Cawshusly they looked under the bed. Yes, there was a man ! They dragged him out. He let them drag. He did not even fire his pistol once. Johnny's father stood ready with a chare to brane him if he resisted. When they had pulled him out they looked at me.

" George Hackett, this is some of your work."

" Well," sade I, " Bess was so surtin she should find a burgler under her bed, I put one there for fun. Don't he look nacheral?—only you've left his boots under the bed."

The burgler was papa's cloes stuffed with straw.

Papa and mamma have been away 4 days, but Bess has telegrafed for them to come back to-night. She says another 24 hours of her bad brother will be the deth of her. I'm doubtful if I get my pony after oll my efforts to be good. There seems to be a pregudice agenst me in this community.

CHAPTER XXI.

HE CONTRIVES TO GO TO THE WEDDING.

I AM not a bad boy any more. Oh, no, I am a wicked, wicked boy these days! Because I go to Sunday-school an to church regular, an try to do gust as the minister does, there 4 I am a wicked, sectreligus boy. Oh, what's the use! I'm sick of trying to be good. When a little incent boy, not nine years old, has the hull town down on him, an the decons an the Sunday-school supertendant, an the preacher besides, wot is he going to do about it? My mind is made up —I'll run away agane. I'll go further than Aunt Betsy's next time. The town will be quiet after I am gone. They won't have any one to slander but the men what's up for President. They seme to be most as bad as I am.

Yesterday was Sundy afternoon; it was a brite, pleasant day, the bluebirds sung—so did the frogs. I asked mamma mite I walk out in the grove to find some traling arbutus. She said yes, if I would be nice an quiet coz it was the Sabbath day.

It was plesent in the woods, there were sevral little girles there picking wild flowers; the brook was deeper than yousal for the spring rains; so I said to Minnie Brown an Lucy Wheeler wouldn't they like to be very, very good children an join the church. They said they would. So I told them I would baptise them

gust as good as the minister. It was Sundy, gust the time; would they let me baptise them?

Annie Spriggs she laughed, which I told her it was rong—they must be very sollum—she an Lizzie could stand on the bank an sing like they ought to. I told Minnie an Lucy they must not be fritened if the water was cold. They said, "No, indede!" Then we all repeted the Lord's prayer very sereous. I was sorry Minnie had on her best blue sash an button kids—the water spoils things so—but she was gust as brave as a little lion; she didn't holler or kick one bit, but looked as sweet as an angel when I led her out; but, oh my, how she did begin to shake, an there wasn't any shawl to put around her, so I hurrid up to baptise Lucy.

I guess I hurrid a little too fast; We both sliped on the slipery stones on the bottom, an fell down, an Lucy strangled like anything an couldn't get up; the streme was a going that fast it swept her away like a fether. It's lucky she was not quite drownded coz the girl hollered like fun, an some men came running, who got her out an took oph their coats an put round her an Minnie, and carrid them home quick as they could.

Nobuddy thought to put anything around me, tho I was shaking so I could hardly walk. Oh, how my teeth chattered ! I've had a sore throte ever since so I couldn't ete anything but gruel and soft stuff; they say it serves me right for being such a wicked boy ! It don't seme to do a bit of good to tell 'em I was not making fun ; I gess I'll give up trying to be a preacher or a doctor ; as soon as my throte is well my plans are layed ; keep dark, my diry, lay low.

Minnie and Lucy are sick in bed —one's got the croup the other's got digestion of the lungs—but I heard Dr. Moore tell Sue, in the hall, they were out of danger ; so what's the use of all this muss?—you'd think I'd turned the world over and all the little girls were falling oph. I thought their parents would like to have them goin the church ; sted of that Betty tells me confidenshally that Mr. Wheeler has bought an offul ugly horsewhip, to give me a tanning the first time I appere on the strete. He is a nasty, ugly, mean ole thing ! Ile's four times my size, witch is cowardly to lick one so much smaller. When Dr. Moore comes up to my room to touch my throte, I'm going to ask him if he won't be my second. I guess ole Wheeler won't dare to punish me when he hears the doctor is on my side.

* * * I asked Doctor Moore would he be my second. He said : " Are you goin to fight a duel, Georgie ?" an he sort of smiled.

I said ole Wheeler has bought a horsewhip, but I think I ought to have the choice of weppons.

He said he thought so too—what would I choose ?

I thought it over, and finally decided he was so much bigger I'd better hide till his rath blew over. So I told the doctor I guessed I'd go to scool by the back lane, so Mr. Wheeler wouldn't get a chance at me.

He said he thought himself " discreshun was the better part of vallor;" but I'm going to carry a few brickbats in my pokkets to be prepared. What with Johnny's mother's loaded pistol and Mr. Wheeler's horsewhip, a little folloe like me don't seme to have any peice of his life. It's a burning shame the way I'm treated by high and lo. If I could deside in my own mind wether sailors or scouts had the golliest times, I could make my preparations akordingly ; I will have to wate until after the wedding to disappear, which is next day after tomoro.

I do hope my throte will get well enuff for me to engoy the spred. It will be a burning shame for a boy with a appetite like mine to have a sore throte when his sister is marrid. I would like to sell out my throte. It is horrid dull being sick. Mamma says what do I thick of poor Johnny having to lay six weeks in bed? I am glad I am not Johnny. I knew better than to clime a tree to get a kite out. I don't kno what to do to pass the time. I am well enuff, only something sticks in my swalloing pipe ; but Betty will not let me dress —she has taken my cloes out of the room ; if I am a good, quite boy, I am to get up tomoro ; I must try to get well for the wedding.

Betty says that fool telegraf

oprator what did not know enuff to let Bess think he bot the flowers, is all rite agane ; he is going to stand up with Bess, an be a nusher in the church. I ast Betty what was a nusher. She sade she was not sure ; she guessed he let the people in the pews. I told her that was a ganitor —those servants are a ignorant set.

Betty is that busy she flys around like a hen with its head cut off; even mamma has been in but once to-day to see me ; weddings are an offal lot of bother. O what fun I'm missing, shut up here with evrybuddy els bizzy as beezs. I herd the doctor and Sue laffing in the hall this morning when he had been in to see how my throte was ; I herd him say:

"His throte is scarcely sore a bit; but I'm going to make him think he is dangerously siek, till after you are safely married to me, my darling. The best place for a boy like that is in bed," an my sister laffed and said : "It's ruther a severe goke on poor Georgy;" then he said :

"He deserves it. If that boy is around, no teling what will happen."

I have been brooding over what I herd ever since. It's a shameful plot to kepe me out of the way. I thought he was my frend. An Sue is in the plot! I dont beleve a little boy was ever treted so before. He gave me ipeak on purpose to kepe me feling sick ! I am to have ipeak an lie in bed, insted of cake, an creme, an salad, an bone turkey, an a good time at the wedding! I thought the doctor was an onest man but it semes he is a fereful hippock-

writ. Never mind, 2 can play at that game.

* * * Well, my sister Sue is Mrs. Doctor Moore now. They are off on their wedding trip to parts unknone. There is pease and quiet in the house now, Betty's legs is geting rested. She said they ached like the toothake when she went to bed for a week beforehand, but Sue she gave her fore of her old dresses, witeh were not good enuff for a bride witch took the ake out wonderful. I had a good time at the wedding after awl. Doctor Moore kept me in bed giving me ipkak once in fore hours witch I spit out evry time ; but I staid in bed an groned an let on I was offul sick an could not swoller I read the whole of "Robison Crueso" an "Famly Robison" 3 times when no one was looking, so the afternoon of the purformunce— witch was very fashnubble at five o'clock—mamma come up an said she was dredful sorry I could not go an so did the doetor but it would not be prudent. O how I laffed when he went out of the room; so the moment they went down I carried out my plan to fool him good like he had tride to fool me.

I could find no close but 1 pare ol old ragged pants I had slid down hill in all winter bec0 because Betty had carried them oph, an my slippers, but I made these do very well because I took a sheet oph my bed, an slid along the hall to a back room climed out on the roof of the kitchen, went down the water-pipe over the fense, down the alley like a streak eause there was no time to lose, along a back street till I was safe, an then I made a bee line for the church. The folks had not begun to arrive yet—I came urly on purpose—but the seckston had unlocked the door to begin to lite up as I krept in wen his back was turned and cut up behind the pulpit where I rapped the sheet around me like it was the minister's white gown and lay lo.

I kept as still as a mouse all the time the hull poplation of the town was poring into the pews. Every seat was crowded, tho I could not see them I herd the rushing an whispering.

After a long, long time witch made my gnees ake, I herd them say there they come! The organ played very soft, Mr. Slocum came in from the vestry, the seremony began. I waited till he came to the place where it says "If any one can show gust cause or impenitent why—" then I bounced rite up in the pulpit with the sheet around me and said very loud and plain—"I can, Mr. Minister."

Such a lot of sprised pople you never saw. Most of them stood up an the women hollered like I was a bear. Sue turned as pail as a gost and grabbed the doctor's arm like she was afrade he would run away. Mamma and papa an the doctor gave a sort of grone—I gess they felt discurridged. While Mr. Slocum was staring up to see who it was, I went on in a hurry for fear they would not let me finish. "I gust want to know if its fair to a little boy to have for a brother-in-law a doctor heartless snuff to pretend he's sick and give him ipkak to kepe him in bed so he can't come to see his own sister got marrid?" O how evry body laffed—xcept our folks. It is very rong to laff in church the way they did. I may be a bad boy but I seldom laff or whisper in church. Doctor Moore he gust looked up and said, "Come down, Georgie, an take a front seat, I promis never to do so again. You beat me evry time." "Very well," said I, "Mr. Slocum you can proseed with the show; but I'll have to be xcused from coming down because Betty hid my Sunday suit—I'll remain where I am." So they got married after all; but some implite pople kept giggling out in the most sollum parts.

I think, dear diry, our famly has learned a leson—not to be ungust to one who may make some mistakes but gencrly tries onestly to be a good boy, I have been treted pretty well since. Nobody scolded a word, but took me in one of the carriages when we went home, an Betty gave me my close quick so I could fix myself up for supper. Lil an Montagu gave me a seat between them and everything nice to ete. I was desprit hungry after so much tea and toste; "Georgie," said Lil, "I see you are as bad as ever," an she laffed an laffed; but I herd the doctor say to Sue that he had changed his mind about their bording with her folks when they came back—they must board at the hotel—I wonder why.

CHAPTER XXII.

IN THE LION'S DEN.

THE doctor says it is urly in the season for the circus crop to come up, but there is one coming next Friday. He has given me 50 cents to go in on. The doctor is a bul—golly good brother. Bully is vulgar; it is all rite when you are playing marbles, but not in a diry. I am learning pretty fast now days; I study the circus bills to learn how to spell. Sometimes it makes me late, but they are more interesting than the second reader. I can spell "akrobat," "summer sault," an sevral more long words of witch I was igrant last week. I think if teachers would have circus posters instid of readers, there scollars would learn faster. It is a combination circus and mennajury. As the bills say, children can study nachural history in all its wonderful varieties of animuls, an advises teachers an parents to give them a holly-day.

To-day I stood up to do a sum in division on the blackbord; the scollars begun to giggle, and the teacher said sturnly:

"George Hackett, 10 marks for misconduck."

I did not know what was up till I looked at my sum. What do you think it was?

A great big elefant with his trunk.

I spose I must a been thinking about nacheral history.

Papa says unless I have a good report this friday, I will not be allowed to go. I hope he will give me money to go, for I had to spend the 50 cents docktor gave me buying Charlie's gack-knife—I mislaid mine for Jimmy's ball, witch was the biggest.

The bucher has sold his pony to the juge for his daughter. Papa said it cost him moren the 40 dollars the pony would have cost to reparo damages when he got home. That is alwas my luck. If enny thing gose wrong about the house, it's Georgie did it. If I was fired from a cannon or a bare back rider I would have an eazier time. I should think grone up folks would be afrade their children would run away an become tumblers or trappeas purformers when they are made so retched at home. There is the dearest little love of a pony on the bills you ever saw, with a boy about my size. I lay awake last night ever so long thinking about it. Offen and offen I have been sent away from table without any pie; offen and offen I have been sent to bed for some harmless aksident. Every buddy is down on me. I try to kepe out of scrapes, but this town is so full of em I cannot help it. Ime laffed at an ridiouled like I was the worst boy on nearth. The town counsel threten to tax my father for 1 boy. The tax on a dog is 1 dollar; they say the tax on me ought to be at least 1000$ a month 12,000 a year.

I am going out of town bout a mile to see the prosession come in. Charlie an me are going together. Poor Johnny, his leg will not be well in time for him to go. I feel real bad about Johnny can't go to the circus. I know gust how he must feel about it. Papa gave me 50 cents last night for doin errans, but I'm afrade I will have to ask Bess' beau what he would do if he wanted to go an had not got the money to go, because I spent mine for 3 plates of ice cream, orange, venilly, and lemon. I was so warm last evening I wanted to see witch kind I liked best, and mamma says I shall not ask for any more.

So I said to that telegraf oprator last evening did he like circusses, an I was very, very fond of them indeed, only I had no money to buy a ticket. I wish I had. He said that was very sad, but he did not offer me any. I tell you if Bess marries him she will be very sorry; he is a miser. I saw him wink at Bess when I refurd to the circus; no gentleman winks. I had finally to tell papa I would weed the garden 2 hours for 50 cents, cause Sam is sick what does our garden; papa agredo. There was a shower to-day, so as soon as I got home from scool I worked like a negro till tea was reddy. O, how tired I was! I thought my back was broke, but Bess said it was not

so hard as hop-scotch on a boy's back, witch shows how much little girls know.

Papa went out after supper to look how much I had done. Would you believe it, dere diry, I had pulled up all the young unions and left the weeds, after he told me so pertikular witch was witch? It seems as if I never would get 50 cents to go to the circus.

* * * Dere diry, I may as well begin at the beginning. The circus has come and went like a butiful dreme. Charley and I went out to meet it. I tell you it was xciting almost as if we belonged to it, running rite alongside of the band-wagon, then we would slow up and let the hull thing go by, rinosserosses, hippotmusses, 2 live elfants, a giraft which has such fun swollowing, cause it tastes good all the way down, a friteful tiger, 2 fereful lions, kept for the purpose of the felloe putting his head into see would they bite, all kinds of wild animals, among which were sevrul pretty girls, lots handcomer than Sue and Lil, purched on the elfants' backs, also on those humpy creatures what gro camel's hair sholls, whatever you call them. It was much finer than the milentary parade last 4 of July. I mist my dinner; I forgot all about it, watching the felloes put up the tents, so when I got home I had gust time to grab a piece of pie Betty saved me; she lent me a dime to buy gingercakes to feed the elfants, and five cents to buy a glass of lemunade, and then I was oph like a streak. I did not think

what might happen before I saw my home agane. Bess was going in the evening long with you know who. I ast mamma was she going, but she said she did not care about it. It was very singler that people can live to be so old as to take no interest in the circus when it comes to town.

So I thought as I past by Peters' grosery I would buy a nounce of red pepper. I mite want it if I ever had to help make catchup. I got some cakes for the elfant too, and then I went in good time to see the animals before the circus begun. It was offul, offul funny to see the monkeys sneeze. I laffed myself most into fits. The keeper said some noty bad boy had put peper in their cage, if he found out who it was he would put him out an have him arested. He was mad as he could be, so I moved away, and went over to the elfants. I gave the large one a ginger-cake; he seemed glad to get it, but elfants, like republicks, are ungrate-ful—(see my scool reder)—for he only just swallowed it when sunthing happened to me, I did not kno what—my teeth was shook like I was playing bones, an bang! I went right up agenst the top of the tent—I xpect that little Georgie would have been no more, only he came down in a carefull of tanbark which they were going to put in the ring. That treehrus elfant had got mad gust because 1 put a leetle teenty bit of red peper in his cake. His keper had a lot of trubble getting him clammed down agen. He shoke his fist at me an said he would not care if I had got my head broke; as it

was, there was a swelled place on it, an I felt kind of queer, so I took my seat and wated for the show to begin. I was sick of being kind to animals.

My headaked some, but I spent a deliteful afternoon. The purformance was first class, no humbug; the clown was rich. I guess I blushed when he pointed me out to the hull crowd and said:

"Why is this little chap like Jonah?"

The ring-master could not tell.

"Coz the elfant throwed him up," was his reply.

Folks laffed, but he must be igno-runt of his Bible—it was not an elfant threw Jonah up, but no matter, I had a good time.

The traned pony was wunderful, and the way those yung ladies went thru those whoops was thrilling in xtreme. Oh, how I envid the little fellows that turned those summersets an stood on their father's heads; how I side because my father was not an acrobat. I believe I can stand on his head gust as well as they did if he would only give up real estate and go into the circus bizness; but he has no ambishun. When I am of age I can chose my own profeshun.

My brane was not idol while the play went on. My mind was made up. No more being the laffing-stock of my native town. No more being called a Bad Boy several 100 times a day. No more scool—no more scold-ing. I would learn the circus trade. After the purformanse was over I went to visit Sue. I hoped she would ask me to stay to supper, coz she bords at the hotel, an if I went to supper mebbe I would see some of those felloes in tites, but they must have had a table to themselfs. I was quite disappointed. I told the doctor if I had 50 cents I would go agane in the evening, but Sue said " No, onse was enuff, it would keep me out too late."

I hung around till I saw them oph ; they went in the evening with the uther young people.

" Now, Georgie, dere, run rite strait home, there's a good boy, so mamma will not worry," said Sue.

I took my time. My plans were lade. I played with the boys in the street till bout 9 o'clock ; then I sliped out to the hotel stable, cut cross lots, come out behind the big tent, where all the wagons stood that were not inside, an I cralled in one of the wagons an pulled a cloth or sumthing over me, so they would not diskover me, an there I lay and waited. I knew they would start bout 2 that night ; I heard the men say so. I meant to get taken along ; then the following day when they diskovered me, I would say I was a orfan boy who wanted to learn the trade ; then they would take me in an put me on the bills as " Little Georgie, the 9 days Wunder, whose ackrobackit purformanse is the marble of the Universe." I must have fell asleep, tho I tride hard to keep awake. When I awoke, the wagon was in moshun. I could see the stars shining, witch made me felt a little homesick, but I kep very still, for I did not want them to find out I was there until we had got a grate ways oph, so they could not send me back. I did not sleep much more ; I was cold, and the wagon jolted, and the driver talked offul to his horses when he got mad ; then I sudenly woke rite up—it was getting to be dalite, I could see the fences an trees. I stirred a little, my lims were so stiff, and then something growled ! My heart stood still, then it went so fast I heard it in my ears like a thousand of brick. I did not dare to stir agen, but my legs aked dredful. Pritty soon I turned my head bout a ninch, an I saw a lion. I was in his cage. He lay there sprolled out, his nose on his paws, his yellow eyes winking at me like he thought it was a good goke. O, my diry, if I live to be as sold as Methusla, I'll never, never forget the roar that followed ! Wurds will not deskribe it. There we were, little Georgie an the lion. It got liter and liter. He gust lay there winking at me like it was fun. I did not see it. If I moved the least bit, he growled. I was pairlized with terror. I said my prayers over and over. I thought of mamma, an Lil, an Betty, how good every budy was to me, an how wicked I was to run away, an the lion he wunk evry time, as much as to say, " Too late ; you oughter thought of that sooner, little Georgie ; wate till my breakfast time. You will only make two bites when I get hungry." O, it was friteful. Time passed very slo. It got to be brod dalite. The lion began to waive his tail an lick his chops. I guess I fanted.

When I come to my senses I was lying on the grass. There were several men around me; the hull prosession had come to a stop. Some buddy had thrown water in my face. I sat up an ast:

"Didn't he eat me up, after all?"

"He came within a nace of it," said a driver. "How in the name of wonder did you come in ole Cicero's den?"

I told him how I crolled in the wagon cos I wanted to learn the trade. All them rough felloes laffed an advised me to go home to my mother. "You've had an arrow escape," said the driver. "We left ole Cicero in his wagon cos he was sick, but how did you get in?" I told him I opened what I thought was a door, I turned a handle an opened the door an shut it—it was a sliding door, an I laid down very quiet. Then he told me how he heard the lion growl, so he looked back and when he saw me he was dead beat. He got me out quicks he could; he had to lick the lion with his whip. So I rode with him upon his high seat till we came to the next town and then I gave up the circus business in disgust.

I arrived home late that afternoon footsore an wery. The folks were regoiced to see their bad boy back agane. They welkomed him like he was the prodigul son. There was cold ham, fride potatoes, an waffles with maple syrup for tea. I think I never tasted such a delishus meal. Our house is a very comfortable house an I don't seem to care about standing on my father's head so much as I did. Pinafore is correct—

"Skim milk maskerades as cream,
 An things are not what they seem."

CHAPTER XXIII.

HE IS DISINHERITED.

UNKEL SAMSON is visiting to our house; he is quite old an febul, and offul funny, only mamma says I mus not say he is funny, becos he is ritch, an a ole bashlor, so mebbe he will leve little Georgie his muney if he is a good boy wile his unkel is here. I kno wot I will do if he dies and leaves me his muney. I will buy the bucher's pony you bet! I wish he would hury up an die, for Bob's father is tauking of buying the pony. He has a very bald spot all over his head, an he is that def you have to screme like a locomotiv whissle to make him here or els you have to go close up to him an holler in a ere-trumpet. Our techer told us we had drums in our eres, but Unkel Samson has to have a trumpet eos his drums arc wore out. It is small at one end, large at the uther, so I tauked in it a little before I went to scool. I said, " Unkel, are you tite ?" He seemed eirprised. " What do you mene, my son ?" said he. " Cos Boss says you are as tite as the bark of a tree ; but some bark is that loos it poles of itself. I would like a dollar to buy Willie Wilkes' xpress-wagon, so I can kepe cook in chips an save kindling-wood, Unkel." Insted of giving me the dollar he seouled an said : " Hey ? hey ? your sister says I am tite, does she ? Young minks ! I *was* going to present her with a hansome silk dress, but I'll think twice about it. Fokes that have no money allus think folks who have oughter thro theirs around like wotter."

He kep snifing and snorting and glared at me through his speks like I was a sho, but he did not give me the dollar.

Foring he was angry I tride to make him plesant agane by telling him in the trumpet, "Mamma said, Never mind, Bess, if your uncle is a miser so mutch the better fur us— there will be more muney to leve us if he don't squonder it :" but he was that out of umor it was like rubbing a cat the rong way—he gumped up and hobbled about mutring to himself so I was glad to take my lunch basket an go to scool by the way of the depo to see wot was going on in the railrode bisness.

So when I came home from scool mamma took me by one sholder,

Bess by the uther, an they asked me wot I said to unkel to make him out of sorts all day. I told them not to wurry, I had not said a thing. " You *must* be careful, Georgie, or the fat will be in the fire," said mamma, very sollum. " Hush ! don't make a noise ! he is aslepe on the loung in the sitting-room—run out dores an play, there's a good boy." I did as I was told, like little boys ought to. The sitting-room windo was open I noticed when I got in the yard ; so I krept up softly an looked in. His specks were on the windo sill. I gust tride them on Towser, to see could a dog see better with specks, but Towser gumped over the fense cos he seen a cat, an wen he come back the specks o whare were they ? I dared not go over the fense to look, for Johnny's mother kepes a pistol loded to shoot me on site. They were gold rimed and I felt quite sorry Towser lost them. Dogs never seme to think how things costs lots of money. Unkel slept on very peaseful, with his mouth open, making a little noise like his throte was a bottle letting the watter run out, with a red banana hankerchef over his head.

It was a great temtashun to try if my fishin-rod was long enough. to tueh the lounge—it was—so I put a blu-bottel on the fish hook an held it over unkel's mouth gust for fun. I did not expect to cach any fish, of course, but my arm got tired holding the rod up, and the hook got in his mouth by mistake, an gust then he snezed in his slepe an his mouth shut up tite. I tried to pull the hook out very softly; the hateful thing would not come, but my unkel did, for I got so fritened I dru so hard I dru him clere oph the lounge. O how he yeld! I droped the rod an cut like a streke of litening out to the barn, where I got lost in the hay so no buddy could find me for a long time.

It was after dark when I crep in the kichen; cook was there stiring a lot of grewel on the stove; when she saw me she looked dagers.

"O you wicked erewel boy," said she, "wot put it in your head to pla your poor unkel such a horid trick? He may dye, the doctor had a friteful time, cutting it out of his tong, which is that tore and lasrated he will have to live on grewel for wekes an wekes, being olreddy old an febul he may dye from the konsekwenses of your crewelty."

"Brigget," said I, in a confidenshal wisper, "if I tell the bucher my unkel is going to dye, don't you think he will kepe the pony for me a little longer?"

She held up her hands a minnit, then she sat down and laffed an laffed.

Georgie Hackett, you do beat the Duch," said she.

I think it was hartless of her to laff, an my unkel sick in the house, but some people have no felines.

It is sevral days since my unkel was taken sick with a fish hook in his tong; the doctor says he is now evanesent. Bess says he is very fathy at me. So to-day, bean able to sit up, he wanted to make a new will; he colled for paper, ink, an his specks. I had got Betty to go over in Johnny's mother's garden an hunt em up, but the glas was gone out of both rims, so I took the glass out of my sister's iglasses, witch is shortsited, and fixed up my unkel's first rate. I did not dare to go in his room, cos he was stil mad at me, but I was that ankshus about the pony I felt I must hear about the will, wether I was to be his air or not, so I sliped in behind Betty when she carried in his grewel, and got under the bed as esy as ennything, an when I had been there a while Squire Gray come an they locked the dore, an put a table by the big chare by the bed an fixed thier ink an a big shete of paper; then my unkel put on his specks, an in about a minit he gave a dreadful grone, an says he:

"My isight is completely gone! Wot *shall* I do? These speks fitted me xackly—I could see thrue em gust as clere as day, an now, all is a cloud—a blur! O dear! O dear! The shock that bad boy gave me must a destroid my isight! I am stone blind. O dear!"

"Maybe the glasses are not clene," said the squire; "let me give em a rub, Mr. Samson."

So he rubed and rubed, but my poor unkel could see no beter.

"This is a fereful stroke," said he. "I shall cut the yung raskal oph without a penny. My sister, too, the hypocrite, to call me a old miser—she shall not have a cent. Nor Miss Bess, my neise, to say I was tite. Yes, squire, my mind is made up to leve my muncy to the home for agged men. None of the Hacketts shall tuch a dollar of 'it. I was quite taken with that little chap at first, but he is uterly depraved—he will go to prison some day; muney will only spoil him. He has lost a cool hundred 1000 $ by his tricks on his old unkel."

Dear me, I am a friteful unforchinate boy! I kep still wile they tauked, an rote, an rote; and then the squire unlocked the door an colled in somebuddy to witness the will, an all was over. It was hot under the bed. I was tired, an the first thing I knew I was fast asleepc. When I woke oll was dark as a stak of black cats; I could hear him snore so I crep out an put my hand very sofly under his pillo where I heard them put the will—it was there—so was his watch an wallet—I took them to my room to give him a good scare, hateful old rip to slander his own litle nevu! I put the other things betwene my matreses, then I struck a lite and held the will in it until it took fire an "crumbled to ashes" like I had read in a novel; I burnt my fingers and let some of it drop, but I put the blaze out quite esy—there was nothing ingured but my new summer wastes witch Miss Pettigru had brought home that day—there was a large hole through the bosom of three of them. I went down an found it was only ait o'clock; my fokes thought I had staid out late playing ball; Betty gave me some cold rice puding an a peace of cake, and then I went to bed.

Bout midnite there was a offul row in the house. Unkel Samson got the hull family up hollering how he had been robbed. There was no more peice that night. His gold watch wurth 2 hundred dollars an 3 hundred in his wallet was a little too much! He was gust wild. There was a windo open, papa thought somebuddy must have entered thro it an took the things.

The more excited unkel grew, the deffer he got, so evrybuddy had to holler in his ere-trumpet; such a time! It semes as if our famly was always getting into skrapes—other famlys don't seem to have so much trubble. Nothing could be done that night, so at last we went back to bed about dalite. Befour brekfast I took the watch and wallet back to unkel. I told him I gessed the thefe got fritened an droped them, but the paper could not be found, so he gave me 10 cents, an said I was not such a bad little boy after all—he could rite anuther will when he got reddy, mebbe he would not leve oll his muney to agged men. Then I spoke to him frendly through the trumpet. I asked him how long pepel of his age generaly lived, because if he had got to die soon, I would be obliged to him if he would leve me forty dollars to buy a pony—I had always longed to own a pony. I told him Bess said he was an old newsance, cause she had to tauk so loud it made her throte soar, but I did not mind speking loud—it was fun to holler in that thing like a telaphone. I asked him did he ever try to hear with his teeth, and did he know Aunt Betsy was mad at papa, and would not lend him money, and said our folks were extravagant. I told him Lil an Montagu had a quarrel, and Docktor Moore would be very poor until he got more praktise, an our cook was not as neat as she might be, an my papa was rather hi-tempered; that papa did not like his coming to spend the summer with us, but mamma said it would be oll right, we would get our pay for it; an how Betty grumbled to me she did not like to button his gaters an wate on him; he was to stingy to give her a doller now an then for her extra work. He seamed to like to hear me talk; sometimes he grinned like he was tikkled; but mamma gave me a teribul scolding this afternoon for letting my tung run—she said I had made mischef enuff—I never can sute all partys.

For instans, last evening that telegraf oprator and Bess were in the frunt parlor; Betty was away, it was her evening out, so my sister said to me:

" Georgie, if themSmith girls come to-nite, remember I am not at home, unkel is il, an mamma is engadged."

So, of course, they came. I ansered the bell; they ast were we to home. I said:

" No; unkel is very sick, mamma is with him wile he writes his will, an Bess told me to say she was not to home, coz she was bisy with that telegraf beau of hers in the frunt parlor—he is teching her about the telefone."

That to-headed yunger girl she snickered rite out, an this afternoon Bess she pulled my hair like enny thing. She said it was alover town about her an the telefone, that she was ashamed to put her head out of dores; so you see how hard it is for little boys to kno what to do under most sirkumstanses.

CHAPTER XXIV.

A FATAL EXPERIMENT.

My brother Montagu has up an gone an dun the most rediclus thing—bot a baby! He pade 20 dollars for it, half enuff to buy me a pony, such a goos, an only a girl. He says if he bot a boy it nite turn out like little Georgie some of these days, which is vary true—one bad boy in a famly is enuff to kepe it bissy. But lately I have ben a xlent child. I have only ben late to skool unce since Monday, this is Wensday, witch is doing pretty well. I have only put a tode in the techer's desk unce this week; it hopped out an made him gump as if as he was a tode himself. I only put burrs in Katy's hair twise; they had to cut some of it oph to get them out. She o not to be so vane of her hair—little girls are very apt to be vane, I am told.

Unkel Samson was going to live at the hotel, but I improved so much, he has konkluded to remane with us for the present. I kepe him posted in what our fokes say, in a low voise, witch they do not wish him to here. He gives me five cents a-day. He is offul curius about what peple say. I cannot plese him better than to tell him oll the names they call him, old skin-flint, old moneybags, old skrue, old liveforever, an such. He says I'i a smart young felloe of my age, au he will not forget to remember me. He stil wurries a good dele over his eyes, cause Sue's glases don't fit him. But to return to the baby, as the papers say. I have seen it—such a site! Why didn't they pik out 1 that could crepe an had hair on its head, an could play marbels with its little unkel? This one is a perfeck idiut I should gudge, besides being a *Injian*—why did they not at leste buy a white child that would be re-speckabel when it grows up? I ast my sister "wot tribe does it belong two?" She said she "guessed the Kickapoos." Such a disgrace to the Hacketts. I suppose they got it be-cause it was chepe, or the last of the lot. Lil hugs an kisses it like it was the swetest thing in babies. She is mad as hops at me because I stuck a pin in it to see was it an Injian-rubber baby. I guess she will be a prise-fiter when she grows up—she struck out an hit me strait in the eye this morning like she had taken les-sons; I was very mutch cirprised the way she did it.

Lil is visiting at home now gust to sho oph that yung one, so I stay out doors a good dele; I do not like to hear it cry, an it is getting on towrd the 4 of July, an we boys have lots of fun in advanse with fire-crackers an uther things of a similar nachur. My 2 married brothers, the telgraf oprater, an Unkel Samson kepe me in pokkit moncy, so I have more crackers than the uther boys, witch makes them very kind an obliging to little Georgie.

There is an old canon on the green in front of the town Hall; it is to be fired oph 100 times the morning of the fourth. But Charlie an I an some more boys have got a lot of powder, an we're going to do somethin funny the circus man did, soon—I guess tomoro. It is a depe secret, but I will tell the, my diry. The circus feller fired a man rite out the canon's mouth. Our cannon is not big enuff to fire a man out but it will fit a baby gust as snug, if the baby is small. So we are going to borro Lil's, it is vary small. But we must not let her kno, she is that careful of it as if it was an eg. We are to watch round after dark when she get's it to slepe and gose down to sit in the parlor, then I am to stole up stairs, rap it in its blanket and bring it down, then we will cut an run. The canon is alreddy loded with lots of powder an about 20 bulits we made by melting up some led pipe we took out our cistern, golly bulits big as hikry nuts. I hope it will not hurt the baby much—I do not think it will—the man that was fired oph was not hurt a partickle. Jimmy Brown is going to borro his granma' fether bed for it to be shot into. After the baby is shot out of the canon I'm going to run home with it, an then we're going up have a bonfire of tar barels witch is splendid fun.

* * * I wish pepel would tend to their own affares an let little boys have some fun once in a wile. Our plan was a perfeck suckces as far as getting the baby out of the house an getting it nicely fixed in the canon. All was reddy to appli the mach, I was gust about to give the word to tuch her oph when we herd such a friteful screming you would a thought some buddy hed got their fingirs smashed, an Montagu's voice shouting "Georgie, Georgie, hold on!" and there was papa an mamma an Sue an Lil an the doctor an Montagu an Betty an the cook a running for deer life an Montagu snached the baby out the canon an Lil fell down an fanted ded away an Sue went into hesterika—such a time about a little rat of a thing that was not worth buying in the furst place! besides, we had not the slitest intenshun of hurting it—we had the fether bed fixed all rite. It semes Betty had been mean enuff to look in the, my diry, to see what I wrote las night, an when she read it she run to see was the baby gone, an when she found it mising she roused the hull house. Such a fuss about nothing. I do not think as much of Betty as I did. She had no rite to look at what I rote, tho Lil says she blesses her for doing it, els what would have become of her presbus, preshus baby.
    * * * The 4 of July promises to be a bizzy day in our visinity. The town counsel fires canon, rings bells, an sets oph 500 dollars wurth of fireworks in the evening—rokkits, roming candels, cathrin wheels, triangels. There are to be 2 picnics in the daytime, ours an the collurd fokses, an the military are to march at ten, an then a womans rites convenshun, an sevral other things going oph like the corks of soda water botles. I xpect to have a glorious time. From five c'klock urly til midnite I shall be as bizzy as a bee having a golly time. I have given papa a sollum promis that I will not play with powder—will not ro within 10 feet of boys who have toy canons—will not fire a pistol—and he has bot me some nice fireworks, to say nothing of about 2 bushel of fire crakers. I can put as many as I plese in a barl an set em oph all at a time. I am sory I cannot have any powder, but papa says he does not wish his only sun to lose his fingers or isite, witch will not be plesant, that's a fak. I am not to throe any crakers at little girls, a notty thing to do, for their dress mite get on fire an burn them up. I can go with them to the picnic, but I am dredfuly undesided wot to do about it. I prefer to see the miltary parade an here the band, but Sue an our cook are making an offul lot of good things for the picnic. When I think of the drums an of marching along behind em, I think I will goin the parade—when I smell the plum cake an the spring chicken roasting, an the boiled ham and gelly, I make up my mind to goin the picnic. I

D

think congres ought to pass an ack making the 4 of July a week long, and then I could go to both. However, we get a good eel of fun in advance. All kinds of shows seem to be perambulansing around the country at this season.

Little Johnny is out agane, but his mother will not alow him to play with me, witch is a grate trial to Johnny. I am sory for him.

About the shows, last week there was another prestydigatator; papa would not let me go to see him. He said such things were as caching as the mesles. Tomoro, witch is the day before the Fourth, at 3 o'klock xactly, there is to be a balloon asenshun from the publick square. A man is going up in it—it will be very intresting. Our techer says it will frustrate the laws of gravity, how a thing that is liter than air won't stay down less you hold on to it. Gas is liter than air, so the man will fill it with gas, clime in, cut the rope, and away he will sore tord the sky like enny thing, hire and hire—O it must be lovely! I would give my new gack-gnife to be abel to ride in a balloon. If he will take me with him I am bound to go.

* * * * * Hooraw! I am going. I gust lade down my pen and streked it down to the hotel, purtending I went to call on my sister Sue, but I kontrived to see the Profesur who owns the balloon, an he said if my parents would give their consent he would be happy to take me up with him. O, wont that be bul—golly? I hope my parents will not be so crewel as to refuse. It will be a novvel xperance witch few boys of my age have had.

Imadgin how funny the world would look when I get up so high the pepel are no biger than flys! I gess I will not ask my parents for fere they will say no. I will gust go an take the chances. It is made of silk, an cos sevral thousand dollars. They ar going to send up a lot of paper ones the night of the Forth, but they are not to be compaired with this. I kno I shall dreme of falling out of it to-night, my mind is so full of it. It would be offul fun to get ahed of the profesur an go up in it alone. I could go where I plezed, perfeckly independent—the furst little boy of my age that ever made the assent alone. Praps I might go as far as Chicago, lite there, an be sent home by xpress. I have alwas wanted to see Chicago. Or if I staid up till the earth turned over I might each a glims of China witch is on the other side. I would like to throw out a sand-bag an astonish a Selestial who was not doing anything but flying a kite when it made him gump 20 feet an lose the string of his kite. I must have a long talk with the profesur to-morro morning so as to lurn how to run the thing.

I got over in their yard when Johnny's mother was down town an huntod an huntod till I found the glases out of unkel's specks, so I took him some iwater in a vial an told him to rub the iwater on at night. So the next morning I had his specks fixed up all rite with the old glases: he could see as good as ever, an he thot it was the iwater, an give me a gold dollar he was so plezed. He has made anuther will in my favor becauze I never tell him what I call him to his back; he says I am an onest little boy. And now, my diry, let me lock the in my desk so that prying Betty will not find out about the balloon and nip it in the bud. Good-night. I must say my prayrs an go to slepe. I hope the Lord will xcuse little Georgie from being such a bad boy, witch he never menes to, only it happens.

[*Note by the Editor.*—We feel quite certain that such persons as have read little Georgie's diary, will feel some regret—in spite of his having been so bad a boy—in learning that his plan of getting away alone in the balloon was only too successful.

Whether he cut the rope which held it, or whether it came unfastened by accident, no one can say, but as the balloon was nearly filled, and the professor about to cut off the supply of gas and go into the car where Georgie was already proudly seated, the huge silken monster gave a sudden leap, and before the dangling rope could be caught it arose beyond reach, and the vast multitude, with one groan of horror, beheld the poor little fellow waving his handkerchief as he was carried up, up with frightful rapidity.

More than a week has passed since that hour, bringing no tidings of the youthful aeronaut, and hope has gradually expired in every breast.

CHAPTER XXV

HOW HE RAN THE BALLOON.

My dere, dere diry, is it possbul I behole the unce agane? It is more than I xpected. Such a time as I have had. I gess Robson Cruso an Jules Verne wish they had been in little Georgie's shoes, but it is a cerious bisness for a small boy of my own age to go up in a balloon alone—more curious than I antispated. It is offul amusing for bout a minit an a half, after that it is simply friteful. I ast Betty was my hair turned white—I thot it would be; I am

postive I shall never be the careles, rash, idol child I was before I took that ride.

Yes, it is deliteful for a minit or so, being in a balloon all to yourself, going up like a thousan of brick, waving your hankerchef and watching the peple growing small, seeing the trane crall along like a snake, the fields an rivers an trees an fenses getting litler an litler—but O, how lonsom a little boy is when he has rozen about a mile an finds he can't stop the plagy thing worth a cent, and there is nuthing around him xcept nuthing, and he is that cold his fingers are num; but he had put a little basket in the car with a fu santwitches an a small bottle of likker of some kind, brandy, I gess, so I took a swallo, I was so cold, an it burnt like fire; an then I thot I had better go up the ropes wile my fingers was limber an cut a small hole or two in the pesky thing, liko I had read of, so it would stop going up tords Greenland. Dear, dear, you would never dreme it was the forth of July in six or seven hours —you would sertanly say it was Chrismas. I am glad now my sisters was not there to holler an screme while I went up the rope, gack-nife in hand, for I might have dropped. It was ticklish bizness, but it was that or freze to deth, so I managed it, sure's your alive! I jabed 2 holes an come down the rope an et a sant-vitch an put his coat around me, which was in the car, an went to slepe.

When I woke up I dremed I was in bed an Betty was tucking me up, but I soon sat up an looked around to see how I was coming on. It was night. The moon shown butiful. I was saling along as nice as you please rite over something that was bright an smoothe as silver; when I came closer, witch I soon did, for the balloon was settling sloly, I saw it was a lake or oshun. Then I felt I was a gone case, domed to be drownded, an his mamma would never kno what became of her only son. I felt very bad. I thot of all the axdents I had got into— how much anxity I had cawsed my dere parents, an I tuged an tuged to throw over a sand bag like the aeronaut had xplaned to liten her, but they were too much for little Georgie. So I resined myself an et 2 more of my remaning santwitches.

Then I looked over the edg of the car an saw a black spot in the shining water. I said to myself " it is a whale;" but in less 'n 5 minits it proofed to be a very small iland about as big as a feild an before I could say "Gack Robsin," that balloon lited rite down on it like a bird on a tree, it dragged along enough to set your teeth on edg, but I gumped out like litening, you bet, an I cot the rope witch I had cut when we went up an tide it round a poor little pine tree gust big enuff to hold it— and there we were! I made it very sucure with lots of nots so it could not play me a trick an get away, an then I got in the car an lay down, for it was warm down there, and I was offul used up and drowsy. When I awoke it was broad dalite. I stood up an took an observashun.

" Hallo, Georgie," said I, " this is a good goke! bein recked on a dessert iland! O if I had my diry what lots I'd have to write in it! I must go to work at once an take an invenstory of what I've got to bild me a hut an subsist on." So I et 2 more of the sanwitches, witch left 1. I was offul hungry; it was a grate temptashun to ete the last but I resisted. I was dredful thirsty, so the first thing was to surch for water. There was lots of it all around the iland, but I was afrade it was salt. There was no other, so I waded in an tasted of it to see where I was, wether I was in mid-oshun or one of the lakes between the United States and Canada, *it was fresh.*

I then set to work at once to save my stores an bild my hut, like Robson Cruso; but alas, a balloon is not worth a penny whissle beside a ship—there were no nails—no sce biskit—no peices of old iron—no salt beef—but I konsoled myself at last by gust making up my mind to use the old thing itself for my house. Then I wanted to bild a picket fence around it to keep off wild animals, but there were no pickets to be had nor no wild animals so far as I could obsurve; so I started out to walk around the iland to look on the wet sand if there were any tracks of cannibulls. I walked a good ways without seeing any tracks or any canoos on the water; then I came back an on my way I found a surtin sign of civilsashun that made my heart beet—an ole tin can, a tomatto can, rusty an bent, but I said I must not waste it, I may need it much; so I filled it with water so I could stand a seege if the cannibulls arriv. By that time I was hot an wery. I climed into the car, et my sole remaining santwitch, drank a little of the water an when I remembered that it was the glorious Forth, an peple were having picnick an marching an firing cannon an having such golly fun, an how I would have no upper, nor sce no fireworks an was lost an starving on a dessert iland, I cride a little, tho I tride to be brave

as folks lost in such places ought to be. I could not help it, though I winked and winked to kepe the tears back, wunking did no good.

I took a nap, an after that I felt some better. I ast myself: "What would Robson Cruso do?"

"Ah," said I, "he would get a stick an cut a noch to mark the days so he would know how many days he staid there."

So I fixed a stick an cut a noch, an after that I spent the rest of the afternoon watching for a vessel to heve in sight.

No vessel heved.

I found some clamshells, but there was no clams in them. I was very hungry. It grew dark an I crept to my car, cuvered myself with the other felloe's coat, an slept sound all night long, I was that tired an home-sick.

Morning came. I made skanty brekfast on watter. My stummick hurt me so I remembered bout the Injuns making their belts titer to stop the nawings of hunger, but I had no belt, so I had to let her naw. I cut another noch in my stick, and walked about trying to find a bread-frute tree, but there was none on that island. There was nothing but sand an little recked pine trees—my stummick aked offul. I thot of the wreckles way in which I had often given my mince-pie to Towser.

I wondered what our fokes would have for supper and were they trying to find little Georgie. Perhaps they were glad to get rid of him when he was such a trial to them. They never would find him, even if they looked a month or a year. O, how little boys plan to run away from nice, kind, comfortable homes, little know how they will suffer when they are cast away on a dessert iland !

I continyud to feel hungry. I thot of a grate many things, speshally waffles an honey. I also continyud to look for a ship. The sun set. I felt worse an worse. I staid by the shore; then all of a sudden I saw one not far oph—a ship I mean. I ran an got my noehed stick an put my hankerchef on it an waved, but I nede not have trubbled; they told me afterward they were stearing strait for the queer thing hiehed to the tree. It was most dark when they dru near, lowered a boat, an three men got in an rode ashore.

"Hallo," said they, when they saw me.

"Hallo yourselfs," said I, very glad to see them.

"Well, I'll be blowed," they ansered "did you ever?"

"Hardly ever," said I, "gust once, in fae. Got anything to eat on bord your ship? My balloon come down here where there isn't even a bread-frute tree or a watter-melon pateh. I'm starving."

An then I came mity near crying, witch I wouldn't for anything, but stratened up, and asked them:

"Are you Merican or British stars ?"

They said they were British tars, who belonged in Canady, but they were saling for Buflo; would I like to go there? So they took me on borde where the captin was eting his supper; he was very polite. He ast

me would I sit right down without seremony ? I did. There was fride fresh fish an fride potatose, bread an buter, an coffy; a most dclishus meal, but I had read how peple when picked up ot to ete but little to begin on, so I refused fish an neggs an potato the 4th time, an ehoked oph on my fifth slice of bread.

He sent the men to take the balloon abord after I told him whose it was, an cost sevral thousan $. He was very kind, an I shall be grateful to him till I am grone up. It took us 4 days an nights to reach Bufflo, but I past the time plesently talking with the salors, who made a pet of little Georgie, not knowing his repu-tashun for being a bad boy. I told them about my sisters, the new baby, the telegraf oprator, an lots of things witch intrested them, an they told me about the see-serpent, the mur-mades, and other wonders of the deep, how to tie a salor's gnot, to go up the mast, an so 4th. I tride to make as little trubble as posbul, but I fell overborde twice in a deep place, so they had to go in for me, an I lost Ben's silver watch in the water, what his mother gave him, but I promised him a better one when I got home. The salors drew an nankor an a ship on my arm in injy ink, so my parents would know me next time I got lost. I felt ever so bad to part with them when we got to Buflo. I huged an kissed them all, an shed a fu teres, they rote all their names in a round robin an gave me for a kepesake. The captin took me to the ears tell-ing the eonduckter I would be pade for when I got there, like I was a

C.O.D. I spose cause I had been in the water so much.

I rode an rode all day, it was gust getting dark when I got off at our stashun. I had made the captin prommis he would not telgraf I was in town, for I wished to sirprise the famly. I sliped oph the last car, an cut for home by a back street, to see what they would say when I came in before they knew it. O, how my heart beet when I drew near; it seemed I had been away an adge—a censury! I went sofly in the back yard an peped in the dining-room windo. My! what lots of good things there was for supper; an there they sat about the table like mummys, not eting enuff worth the cooks trubble. Mamma had a hankerchef to her eyes, Bess was pail an silent, Betty was snifling as she handed the toste to Lil an Montagu—such a set! So I bounced rite in the open windo like I was a Ingy-rubber ball, an I said :

"You'd have a beter appetite, you fokes, if you had been cast away on a desert iland like I was. O, my, how hungry I am—give me suthin to etc."

Good grashus—but my pen fales me—I will draw a curtin over the scen. Only one thing strikes me as pecoolyer—bad boys' famlys seem gust as glad to get them back when they have been lost as if they were not such dredful children. But I have had a leson, an I mene to try hard to be more worthy of Betty's strangling me half to deth pretending she is hugging me. Even that little redicklus red baby laffed when it saw its unkei Georgie.

P.S.—It's well the captin took charge of that balloon; the aeronaut has sude my father for seven 1000 $, but now all papa will have to pay will be for the paches that will have to be sode on where I cut holes with my gack-nife. My sisters are going to give the captin a silk flag, an a nice watch to each one of my frends, the British stars; they are golly (my sisters).

CHAPTER XXVI.

HE RUNS A LOCOMOTIVE.

UNKEL SAMSON is that tired of staying to our house he has gone away. He went off huffy, without giving me a pony to remember him by. I felt very bad the day he went away at parting with my unkel before he had bot me that pony. If I had him I should not have missed my unkel at all. He did not intend going before autum, but unxpected sircumstanses hurrid his departyour. It is vaka- shun now, an we boys have plenty time to play, so we had a show in Charlie's father's stable, two afternoons, admishun 3 cents, grone ups half prise. Charlie was a munky. Harry was a bear, and I was the Grate What Is It. We had uther animuls an sevrul side shows. I went to the barbers an had my head shaved, an then Charlie painted my face an hands dark brown. He had to use real paint what was left from the fense cos we had nothing els, so you may gess I am a site. It will take all summer for it to ware off, so I cannot go to church. I don't kno myself when I look in the glass. Bess says it is 2 bad to eat at the same table with a little culured boy. She thinks I ought to wate an eat with Betty, which Betty despises to sit at the table with a What Is It, so mamma lets me come when there is no cumpany.

But unkel got out of temper gust because I borroed his set of false teeth to make me look more like one, when he was taking his nap, and droped them in Charlie's fokes well when we were getting a drink. The day was very hot. I did not mean to drop them. It is sixty feet deep, an' the man that went down could not find them. They were gold, and eost lots of money, an unkel most starved while he was having another set. I felt offul sory for him when he was eting, but he would not aksept any appologies from such a bad boy. Gust as soon as he got another set of nickel-plated, or gum-elastic, or whatever they are, so he would look fit to be seen, he ordered a dray an had his bagage tooken to the hotel. You see Harry had a pet donky which we purtended it was a baby elefant, so I had to borro my sister's cashmere sholl unknone to her to spred over it. Of coarse it had to have a trunk els the show would a been a ded falyure, an there was not another thing would anser but my unkel's ere-trumpet, witch did first rate when we got it fastened on, witch was a job. When he had made it some biger legs out of Charlie's father's horse's rubber blanket and tied the red sholl around it, it was as cute a baby elefant as you ever saw—most as good as the fildelfy baby. It was wurth 3 sents to see it. But unkel could not hear much for sevral days, cause the donky forgot he was a elefant an tore round an gammed his trunk all up like a reglar bagage smasher. That an the teeth together was a much for his pashuns; he was so rathy he made my mamma cry.

I don't kno as he would aktually gone away, only we took his best silk dressing-gown that he got in Japan for Charlie to dress up as a Turk with banana hankerchef for a turban, an a little paint got on them by aksident when we tiped the paint-pot over in the stable witch ruined the dressing-gown—a grate pity for it was a buty, all silk flowers. Charlie ought not to have been so careless. We had a golly show, you bet. There were 13 boys an 3 girls came to it. We took in 50 cents witch we aregoing to give to the hethen. For my part I don't mind unkel's going to the hotel to bord. Betty told me privately she was tired of him. He says I have lost a forchin by my misconduck, but I don't kno as I need a forchin; I have a good deal of fun an plenty to eat; an I did not mene to make him angry when I fastened my sisters best switch to the bald spot on his head with shumaker's wax—I only wanted to see would he look like a Chinaman, but some people cannot take a goke. Bess says I have ruined her switch, switch cost 10 $. What for does she ware one, then? Girls would be more comfortable this hot weather if they dressed their hair like mine. If a girl cannot spend 1-2 her time fixing up for her beau she don't care to live. I told that telegraf felloe that Bess las night fore she came in the parlor had gone up stairs to powder an put on her bang, an tuch up her ibrows—that her hair was coming out dredful. I xpected 'she would be almost bald; how she used to freckel till she used lemon-glycerine. I was just going to tell him about her being trubled with corns when she came in.

To-night the door-bell rang an Betty was gone to the store; my sister looked through the bliuds an said :

"Oh, Georgie, it's those new fashnuble peple that I called on last week. There's a olful nice yung man in the family. Betty is out. You look gust like a little culured water boy. I tell you what you do—you go to the door an show em in in stile, an then you stay out of the room. They will not be here long."

I opened the door with a flurish like those waiters at the hotel, an bowed them into the parlor very polite. Then I staid away like Bess told me to. Only it was lonesum in the sitting-room, so pretty soon I slid into the parlor an went to looking thru the stereskope.

"George," said my sister in a lo voice, " retire."

"What for?" said I. "Oh, I forgot. Never mind, they will see I am your little brother, if I am a mulato. You cannot pass me oph for a waiter-boy."

Then they looked cirprised, an my sister had to xplane how I had painted myself an it wouldn't come oph, an they said :

"Ah, yes; they had heard about me—wasn't I the yung gentleman who had gone up alone in a balloon, an so forth?"

I spose the hull town talks about me coz I have had a fu aksidents happen to me. I'm a laffing stock wherever I go. I hate to go down street, all the felloes goke me. They don't call me ennything now but the What Is It. I wish this paint would come oph. I am going to get Betty to scrub me with sand.

* * * It is no use; my fun has gone up the spout. I'm that ridiculed, an goked, an laffed at, I cannot stand it. I think I will run away to my Aunt Betsey's an stay till it wears off. It does not pay to be a What Is It week after week. Of course my aunt will not know me. I will hire out to her as a little cullurd boy to pick blackberries for his borde. I hope by the time

that scool begins in September I shall be white agane. When I go down street the felloes offer me coco-nuts. Doctor Moore calls me the missing link. They say they are getting up a subskripshun to pay my passage to send me to Darwin; they think they are offul smart! I went to the concert, an they were not going to let me sit with my own sister, but up in the gallery. I am disgusted. The next time Charlie gets up a show, he may be the What Is It hisself.

* * * It is coming oph in spots, and they call me the leppard. It is friteful what konsequences may hapen when you don't mean to have them. I have alwus thought I should like to be a engineer if I was not a salor or a skowt. I like to be around the depo; the fellows there are very kind to me, tho sometimes they teze me a good eel. They have offen laffed at little Georgie's mistakes when they heard of them, but now they laff out of the other side of their mouth. Bill Bellows is a enginere on a frate trane that stops here frekwently; he is one of my gratest frends. He would take me on his engine when he was on the side-track wating for the passenger trane an answer all my questions very good-natured; so I was on with him yesterday, an I ast him how he started her, an he showed me.

"You could almost run her yourself, couldn't you, bub?" he said; and then he an the fireman they reckoned they had about time to go in the saloon on the corner and get a paper of tobacco before the passen-gers was due, so they went. Bill helped me down, an told me to run over into the stashun house so as not to get into trubble; but I wanted to see how the old thing went, so I gumped on when he was not looking but was drinking a glass of soda-water, an I pulled out the little thing he showed me to make her go, an before I knew it she was going. I scremed to her to stop, but it wasn't no use; the nasty thing only went the faster. The enginere an the fireman run out—you never see how pale they looked through the dirt on their faces—they ran like mad, but the locomotive beat em as easy as enything. I saw the fokes running an waving their arms, an I thought of the day I went up in the balloon, an I felt offul. An then I was rite out in the country, taring along with all these frate cars behind me, an I remembered the passenger train would be due in five minutes, an I was that fritened I couldn't think to stop her, for I was going rite strait towards it, an I knew it was coming tords me, an I thot to myself "what a smash!" It was worse than the balloon to think of all the people on the other trane. I cride an sobed, but that did no good. I wished I had stade away from the depo like my mamma said I must. I thought of all my bad axions, and how Unkel Samson looked when I told him I had lost his teeth in the well, an how vexed Bess was when I was under the piano that moonlite night last week when he ast her had she ever loved before, and she said "never," an I hollered out, "O, what a whopper! Bess, remember that time you took a buggy-ride an the horse ran away?" but all this time I was flying on like lightning till I knew I had gone six miles, coz I was coming to the next stashun—I could see it, an the passenger trane standing there, an the people on the platform—O, it was an offul moment!

And then, about a minit after that, we shot rite by like a canon going oph—there was a dredful riping, taring noise, an something hit me on the head like it was mad at me.

Betty has told me all about it, for I knew nothing for some hours. When I came 2 I was on a bench in the depo, with the hull family around me. Doctor Moore said I was suffring with conclusion of the brane, but he guessed I would get over it —I was hard to kill, witch was a pity. Bess told me he ot to be ashamed, which was good of her, seeing how I treted her, getting under the piano that time. I will never, never do it again!

It seems when Bill saw his trane running away he dashed into the stashun an said to the telegraf sprator, "telegraf quick as litening down to Hartford to switch her off," witch he did, for he did not know I was aborde, an if he had it would have made no difrence, as Bill says, fond as he was of me, when it was a question of 30 or 40 lives he could not hesitate. They just barely managed to switch her off in time, keeping the passenger trane there until I whizzed by an ran into the fratehouse down the road.

Everyboddy thought I would be crushed to attoms, but I only got a big bunch on my head an a black spot on my arm—I was piched into a wagon loaded with cotton bales for the mill quite providenshal. The hull town is grumbling coz I was not killed—they say I am a dangerous nusanse, an they wish I had a been. The engine is a total reck. 7 frate cars smashed and lots of frate destroid.

* * * I had just rote that much when Betsy steles up to tell me they have held a town meeting an resolved to put me in jale. She says it is in riting:

"Whereas, George Hackett is an incorrigabul bad boy, and the caws of grate loss and damidge to the town in menny ways, there 4 resolved that he be incarcerated in the county gale for 6 months so that pease an order be restored to a aflicted community.

"Resolved, that our sympathy be xtended to his famly, but that no mercy be shone to the culprit."

Betty says she tells me, so as to give me a chance to eskape, as they will not come for me until morning. So farewell, my diry, a long farewell.

I have not decided whether to go to Buflo on borde that vessel whare the British stars will take me in, or to stay and go to prison. It semes hard that a little boy who never in his life ment to do harm—an unforchinit child who has met with a few aksidents—should have to go to gale. Betty has sollumly promised to bring me a basket of pie an cake every day. I suppose it will not be a bad place for the paint to ware oph an my hair to grow. I suppose I shall have to wear striped cloes. Well, I must resine myself.

P.S. It is all a hoxe. The doctor got it up to friten me. They cannot put me in gale, but they say they will take me up for steeling if I ever try to run away with a frate train agane. I never will. i such lesson is enuff. I shall never do anything bad from this time onward. Bess is going to have a crokay party to-nite. I wish I could hire somebuddy to tell her that we used up all the balls of both sets to make a Turkish bazar out of Charlie's picket fense the time we had the show.

CHAPTER XXVII.

HE VISITS THE FALLS.

At last I am a very good boy. I have tole johnny's mother how sory I am he was so careless as to break his leg. I have repented in dust an dashes what I did when I let the mouse out, an those silly girls set fire to the town hall, such an xpense to the tacks-payers. I could not be indused to steel a ride in a baloon, not if it was ophered to me for nothing. No, indede! I am very much reformed, even my sister Bess says she hardly knows her little brother. The reson is I have met with a friteful axdent witch might easily have proved fatul only it didn't hapen to; it makes the tears come in my eyes when I think how bad my mother would a felt if her only son had xpired of drowning in that dredful manner.

You see, dear diry, I have been taking a summer trip with my parents. As mama said, Lil an Lue were out of the way, an Bess was engaged (telgraf oprator) so she thot she might rest on her roars; she felt sort of worn out with her family cares, speshly Georgie, witch she had never fully got over that week he was lost in a baloon, an she thought papa might take her travelling for her health, so he suckjested Niagara falls, witch we all sade would be splendid. Only Bess, she up an declaired they shoodn't go unless they took me to. She cood not be risponsabel for what hapened if I staid at home in my father's absence. Bess is golly; she knows whats what. I gust went out an stood on my head in the yard when they said they suposed they'd have to take me. Towser come up an wagged his tale, an I said, "Towser, keep quite an lay lo, an you shall go to," witch pleased him very much. We started the next evening, after dark, to go through in the night. Towser an Bess, her bow, an some others went to the deppo to see us oph. It was a litening xpress that stopped to water, so when it come in like a streke, mr mma she began to stir an worry like women will.

"Georgie, Georgie, you'll be left! Where *is* that boy? O dere! If this is the way you're going to akt, I wish we had not come. Don't you never wait till the cars is in motion agane before you get on board, my son."

"It's all right, mamma," replide I, when we had tooken our seats an was fixed comforable, and had gone a few miles. "I only stopped to tie Towser to the axl of the hind car—he wanted to come along offal bad." Then she lened back, looking kind of sick, an began to screme, "Stop the trane! stop the trane." "Such a hubbub!" "What is it?" "Whose hurt?" "Pull the bell-rope!" "We're run into!" "There's ben a colishun!" The women hollered, the men turned pail, sevrul of them pulled the rope, the trane slued up, the conductor rushed thro.

"Who stopped this train? What's up?"

"My son has tide our dog to the last car," gasped mamma. "O, save him, we have had him years, and love him derely."

That impertnant conductor looked at me like he wanted to ete me.

"I wish it was the boy was tide to the axl," he muttard; but he had his trubble for nothing, there was no dog left worth stoping the litening xpress for, only a peace of rope and 1 ear. I was sory for Towser, who was a very faithful dog. I thought he would enjoy the trip.

If I snored like some people do, I would never travel. Papa says it is an imposishion to pay three dollars for a secktion in a sleeping-car and then not be able to sleep. This person was in the upper berth, next to mine, so I tride to stop him, that my poor mamma might get some slepe. I reached around, an' stuck a pin in his arm up to the head; and then I laid down so quick and fell asleep so hard, when he bounced out in the isle he didn't know what hurt him. "Porter! porter!" he yelled, "somebody's ben trying to rob an' murder me." "Nonsense," said the porter, "you've had the nightmare." "'Cause he's snored himself horse," said a felloe on the other side. At that sevrul stuck their heads out an' laffed, an' he climed back agane an' lade quite for a nour or so.

I was offal thursty like I always am when I travel, so gust as all was quite, I had to call out, "Porter, please bring me a drink of water." He brung me one, but I continued thursty. I did not like to disturb the people agane calling the porter, so I gust sliped out very soft an' went an' helped myself. Then I came back very still, an' crep' in bed like a mouse, when there came such a succession of screeches right in my ear I was fritened out of my senses, an' I was pushed out and fell down in the ile like a thousand of brick.

Every blessed sole in the car had their heads out. The porter picked me up an' shook me like he mistook me for a dusty coat, an' a woman who had her false teeth under her pillow, an' was bald-headed, sobbed and cride, and said she thought I was a man. It semes I had mistaken my berth. But everybody got to slepe agane after a time, an' all was peace an' sweet dreams until it gru daylite. It is very rong the way men sware when they are mad—the ladies do not do it. The men in our pallis sleeping-car said offul bad words when they went to dress theirselfs that morning, gust for nothing only the poor porter had mixed their shoes up in a perfeck muddle—nobudy had his own or 2 alike. The porter said they were all right after he blacked 'em, witch made some of them look savidge at poor Georgie, who was dressing his self, as meek as Mary's little lam ; but, as the books say, alas ! there is a grate deal of ingustice in this world.

I regret that Towser did not live to see the Falls. Words fale me. They are extraordinarily immense in size an' their roar can be heard for miles. There is a rainbow an' sevrul objecks of intrest in the visinity. There are 4 sides to the falls—the outside, the inside (where you go under), the Canady side, and the American side. There is a picture of them in the gography, but it fales to convay an idea of the thundering noise they kepe up night an' day. I think if Mister Barnum could take them abroad like he did Tom Thumb, an' exhibit them in all the grate cittys, they would prove very instrucktive to little boys, shoing the works of Nature to the best advantidge. But the hackmen are exorbitant. Pa says their charges are more astonishing than the Falls. He need not take the hackmen along.

There was a frenchmen going to cross over on a rope the day I got there. Mamma said he must be mad, but he did not seem to be ; he was good-natured enuff when I saw him. She would not go, and she begged papa not to lose sight of me one single instance—no, not one—if she would let me go to see the frenchman walk the rope. He promised he would hold on to me like wax, so she let us go, while she lade down and took a nap, on akount of being disturbed at night on the sleping-car. It was golly fun, very exciting indede, to see him go over in a basket; go over in his stocking feet with the British an American flags—so at last he said who wood like to take a nice little trip over in a wheelbarrow? He would agree to take a person safely over, or pay him $500 if he failed to do it, and they got killed. I thot it would be nice to go over safe, or to get the money, if I didn't. Papa was bizzy talking with a man he didn't expect to meet at the falls. I saw he did not notis, an I sliped quitely away up to the performer an whispered to him I was reddy to go.

"Sonny," said he, "you won't be sorry, for you will be famous all your days. Just think! the only little boy that ever rode across the rapids in a wheelbarrow !"

So I got in, and he gave me two little flags to hold, an he said :

"Shut your eyes tite, or you will get dizzy; trust all to me ; your gust as safe as if you were in a feather-bed at home."

But that nasty plice offiser come along and gerked me out, an asked where my parents were—he was going to have them arrested for Cruelty to Children; an papa come running an wanted to whip the frenchman. So I lost my ride. It was too bad. Mamma said she would not trust me out of her sight agane a single minnit while we were at Niagara. It was a narro escape ; it made her shudder. The next day we bought a pinquishon for Bess from the skwas, an a bow an arro for me, and we went on Goat Island, but I saw no goats. You wood not beleve how fast the water goes by. You throw in peaces of grass an paper, then you will see. There was a lady there, dressed up to fits, she carried a pug dog with a pink ribon, offal cute, an she let me talk to him an hold him a little while to rest her arms. I don't know how on earth it happened, but gust when she was looking at something mamma pointed out to her, Nellie (that's the pug) fell into the water. I gust saw a pink bow about half a second, then I saw no more. You wood have sposed it was a baby the way that woman went on! If papa had not held her tite, I do beleve she would have gumped in after her. As it was, she went into histeriks, and had to be taken to the hotel.

"You careless boy," said mamma, "that's the second since we left home."

I almost cride myself—such a cunning little crechur, fawn-color, with a curly tail an' a funny black nose ; but I satisfide myself that the water went about a mile a second. Sackrifices have to be made in the course of science, my teacher says.

But it is time, my diry, that I tole you about my own hairbreath escape. I have been in dedly peril. It makes my blood run cold to think of it. Fu boys of my age can relate such an experiance. The Falls are grate— very grate—immense—but I do not care to visit them agane, espeshly without a life-preservcr. On the 2d day, when the fish came on for dinner, it reminded me it would be fun to fish in the river, so I lay lo until mamma took me to her room an' told me I had got to read while she took her sighester, witch she does evry afternoon. Pretty soon she was aslepe. I looked out the windo—the sky was blue, the sun was bright. I longed to be oph. I crauled out on to the roof of the piaza, sliped down a pillar, bought some tackle in a little store across the street, an' run away. I took a long walk up the river where the water floed very quiet and slo. There I sat down an' fished. I did not cach anything, so I went on up a considerabul ways higher, till I came to a mill, where there was a small boat tide up to a little dock. No one was looking, so I borrocd the boat. I thought Ide row across an' see if there were more fish on the Canady side. When I had pulled out a short distance the mischef got into the plagy boat: it whirled around, something pulled the oars out of my hands just as if they had reached up a pair of hands and gerked them away. I began to go down stream so fast I thought of pug an' her pink ribbon, but I did not seme to take the same intrest in sience this time: I forgot to calkulate how swift I was going, an' begun to wonder how little boys felt when they got drownded going over Niagra Falls.

I felt sick to my stummuik, and wished I was back in mamma's room reading quietly like a good boy. * * *

I see by the daily papers they had quite an exciting time at the Falls that day. Some men saw a small boy in a small boat taking a solitary ride down the rapids; they ran an' shouted, but it did not do a mite of good. Other folks saw the boat an' shouted an' run, but that did no more good. The bravest man in the world could not help that little boy. On an' on he went. Oh, it was horribul, horribul! He held out his poor little arms to the peple on shore. He shut his eyes an' said his prayers; he promised he would honor his father an' mother, an' mind his sister, an' kepe out of skrapes, an' become a modul boy. I guess Providence heard little Georgie, an' concluded to give him one more chance. If all bad boys died early there would be none left to grow up and become Presidents of the United States. Little Georgie's boat ran on a sharp rock and stuck there. It stade there quite a while.

The peple, hundreds of them, stood on the shore an stared at him

as if he was a sho. A man shouted to him to hold on; that did lots of good. The sun was setting, he thought how terribul it would be to go over in the dark; he beleved he could see his dear mother waving her arms and throing kisses to him; o how he wished he had always taken her advice; how sad it would be to never see Lil's baby any more. He wished he had not tride to shoot it out of a canon. Such were some of the poor child's refleckshuns.

I don't eggsackly know how it was done, but little Georgie was saved. The frenchman did it. They shot a rope across the river and made it fast, both sides; then the frenchman come out on it, hand over hand, right over the boat, an he sliped a nose over Georgie an told him to fix it under his arms an kepe cool; then he drew him up an tole him to shut his eyes an keep still—heed do the rest; and he did it.

Such a scene! Such hurrahing an shouting, an mamma hugging the akrobat like he was her long-lost brother, an fainting ded away, an the peple bringing her an me into the hotel. Papa gave him a check for 500$ on the spot, an said he was a brick; but papa tole me privatly he thought it cost more to raise me than I was worth—he had read that it cost 5000$ to bring up a ordinary boy, but I had cost him five times that already, besides what it had been to other folks, an the bridge I blowed up an the town hall.

I don't think he ought to have scolded me the very night of my myrackulus escape, but that's the way with ungrateful parents. Mamma had sevrul fainting fits that night; the doctor said the shock mite have killed her; she would not get over it in a long time. Of course I should not have taken the boat had I not wanted to do a little inocent fishing, to cirprise my father with some fish —he is very fond of them, an the water looked so smooth and still. The worst of it is I lost my new gack-knife—it will never be found, for I dropped it where the water goes offul swift.

We came home as kwick as we could the following day, an mamma is now lade up. It was foolish for her to be so shocked before she knew if I could be rescued. It seemed to be quite easy for the frenchmn to rescue me; tho, of course, if the boat had not cot on a rock that would have been the last of little Georgie.

So, now, Bess has made me promis to reform, and I hav—thurroly. And as you, my dere diry, are now full, I will bid you a long farewell until I get another.

"My pen is poor, my ink is pale,
My love for you will never fale."

LITTLE GEORGIE.

N.B.—Folks are offully xcited about the eleckshuns. Papa is one of the counters, and me an Johnny have made up a plan to hav some fun. I wont tell wat it is until it comes oph. Weve got a tar barl an a lot of matches out behind the barn. Mebbe, if we can't havo a barbecue we'll roast Mooly's calf, but don't you let on. We want to cirprise our famlys.

CHAPTER XXVIII.

HE TAKES PART IN THE ELECTION.

I DON'T know as I shall sosheate with little Johnny after this; he is too yung for me, an' Lizzie says she winders I will go with a little boy of his age—I o to go with older boys. She is nearly 'leven, han'some as a picture, such grate black eyes, such stile! She is bang up, I tell you. She is visiting to our house, witch mamma says is all rite; she is older than Georgie, an' can kepe out of mischif. I cannot cut oph her hair, because it is olreddy cut oph. So we are grate frends. She aperes to be very fond of me, an' I am offul fond of her. She has a way of waring her bang that is killing. I asked Betty last night, conlidenshal, what made my heart go so quick when Lizzie come in the room, an' she laffed an' laffed like it was a very funny question to ask an then she said: "Don't you know, Georgie," an' I said, "No," an' she said, "Why, you little goose, you are in love;" but she promised she would not tell 'cause I never told when she gave her young man cake in the kitchen. So it is a secret between me an' Betty till I get a chance to explane matters to Lizzie who is going to stay a cuppel of weeks, witch gives me time. Doctor Moore gave me 50 cents to hold his horse when the man was sick, an' I went round with him; it run away and smashed the sulky some, an' he had to sell the horse, but I was not much hurt, so I did not give him back the 50 cents. I bot a beautiful bokay with the money, and give it to Lizzie. I watched her to see if she would blush, a sine, Betty said, she returned my love. She did not blush, an' I am afraid it is because I look so funny with a long strip of sticking-plaster acrost my nose where the skin was barked when the horse ran away, but wot is a girl's love wurth if she cannot like a fello gust as well with a peace of sticking-plaster? The way she laffs when she looks at me hurts my feelings depely. I am sorry I squawndered the 50 cents on 1 so hartless. There is a boy across the way who is almost grone up—he is twelve, an' has a freekeled face an' a new blue suite, quite nobby, so I am cut out. Well, let her go. I shall be stujusly pelite to her no more. Besides, my mind is now so taken up with the

coming cleckshun I have little time to stay in love. It was pleasant while it lasted.

There is grate excitement in our town. You would hardly know it; all the flags flying, an' bands are playing, an' torchlite processhuns, an' speches in the new hall. It is my idea, there is so much fuss about it, that one or the uther candydats will be cleckted sure, perhaps both. I hope they will. It wood be too bad to spend so much money for nothing. My father says it is well for our boys to begin to understand pollytics when they are yung—that the fuchur depends on yung America. I agre with him. I have did my best to help along the good cause. Papa says if evry 1 had done as much as little Georgie, there wood be no country left to save.

This is high prase but I deserve it. I have not been idle a single evening of the champagne. I have yelled myself hoarse; have marched in the crowd, have fired oph the cannon on the square, have fot every boy of my sise or smaller in the naborhood, have helped the men lug stuff to make bonfires. To be sure I have made a fu mistakes, an met with some acksidents: but I guess the president will get cleckted after all.

My sister Bess an sevrul other of our fashnubble young ladies took up a subskripshun to get a first-class banner for the Volunteer Bonton's, what were going to parade in the torchlite processhun. It was 12 feet long, made of silk, with their name on to it in butiful embrordered letters witch the ladies worked—a splendid flag you bet! The proceshun came oph last night. The Voluntcer Bontons met in the hall in the afternoon to receve the banner from the fare hands of our hansomest girls. Little Georgie was the hero of the occashun. He was put up on a platform, where the ladies were all dressed up to phits, to make a speech, and hold the banner till the captin came up an made *his* speech an took it from the hands of the brave little feller (that's myself) witch made some of the ladies weep, they were so affected when I took out my hankercher witch hapened to be full of snuff, so that the captin, every time he began about the American neagle, would call it the grate American chin-eagle, or chuggle, or ker-chuggle, or some such nonsense, gust as if there was any bird knone as the ker-choo-choogle, till everybody laffed an clapped an scremed so you couldn't here a word, an the poor offisir was as red as fire an his ise full of tears so he couldn't see the flag staff witch I was wating for him to grab hold of, but seesed my sister's silk umbrel an retired with that. The people did not kno about the snuff; they thought he had taken the episooty suddan. They gave him three cheers, witch o to made him happy an not say he would ring little Georgie's neck when he cot him outside.

The grate torchlite proceshun came oph to order. It was a fine affare bout 2 miles long or more, cause it went round the block so there was no end to it. There were sevral hundred people in it, the torches looked magnifiscent; the music was butiful, only the big drum was out of tune—some notty boy had made a hole in it an put a kupple of cats in—the cats were good, but the drum was spoild. He never try that on agane.

Rite behind the Voluntcers came a squadroon of little fellors on horseback, with sashes an torches, quite a pritte sight. They would have been a compleet suckcess, only I was so unforchunate as to get my torch too close to the new silk flag, which was being prowdly carried by the Volunteers. I had a curyosity to discover if silk would burn. I was cirprised to find *it would.* In about 2 seckunds it was in a fereful blaze, an in about 2 more, that banner, where was it? I almost cride, after Bess an all the rest had tooken such trubble.

It was a damper on the whole affare. I had to take to my heels, or rather to my pony's heels, cos they thretened if they cot me they would put me in the tar-barrel they were going to make a bonfire with. I tell you, my diry, I lade lo the rest of the evening. I said to Johnny:

"Who cares, les have a show of our own."

He said, "Agrede."

I said, "You boost me, Johnny, an Ile get in the back windo of the Town Hall—its open—theres a lot of fireworks thare for the grand cclebrashun next week. Ile get a fir——."

He boosted me, an I climed in without much dificulty an handed out 3 duzzen large size rockits, about a hundred Roman candels, a lot of cathrine wheels an serpents, everything I thot we could manage. Then we borroed the ganitor's wheelbarro an took them over to the depo, a big boy helped us an we had a lovely time. The hull town left the bon-fire to see wot wos goin on by the depo, only something we didn't know how to manage bursted up an hurt sevral peopel. I was blone up, but I came down on top of a frate-car, witch shook me up a little, my nose bled, there is a bump on the back of my head an a little powder in my face witch makes Lizzie laff at me more than ever, but I am safe an Johnny an I are going to have some fun tomorro or next day.

My father has gone to a naboring villedge to hear some grate speker in the open air. He said the folks were going to have a barbecue to finish up the fun. I asked him what was a barbecue. He said it was rosting an ox hull with plenty of hard cider an uther good things to be et an drunk out of doors so as to make it more golly. I wanted to go along, but he said he would not take such a looking boy—besides I had been very bad last night, he wood leave me behind for a punishment. I felt very lonesome, so I whistled for Jonny to clime over the fence when his mother was not looking. I said:

"Johnny, if we had a nox we could have a barbecue all to ourselfs—wouldn't that be fun?"

He said it would be offul fun only we had no ox. So then I said:

"There is more ways than one to skin a cat—come out behind the barn an I will sho you something, Johnny."

This was about 4 o'clock. About six my mamma saw something brite shining before she lit the lamps. Everything was all red an as lite as day. She ran to the windo an screemed:

"O Bess, Bess, the stable is on fire!"

But she was mistaken. It was only a big fire behind it witch me and Johnny had made to have our own privat barbecue.

It is true the corner of the cowshed had got in a blaze, but the nabors put that out.

"The cow is safe," said Bess, "but o dear, where is the cunning little calf?"

"What's that?" cried mamma, turning pale. "Georgie, you notty, good-for-nothing, cruel boy, tell me this minnit—O you wicked boy!"

"It's only me and Johnny having a barbecue," I answered.

"A what?" she cride.

"A barbecue, mamma. If big folks roste an ox I should think little ones mite roste a teenty weenty calf. Its most done now—wont you all stay an have a piece? We're got a lot of cider, too, out of Johnny's sellar. Were going to do it up in reglar stile."

"Did you roste the poor thing alive?" shrieked my sister.

"Why no, Bess, don't you see we rosted it dead?"

Its strange how little some girls know. It was unreasonable for mamma to make such a fuss about a miserable little calf. Johnny was sent home, an' we neither of us got a taste of our barbecue; but papa could stuff down all he wanted, I dare say. The older I grow the more injustice I see.

N.B. Johnny told me in a whisper this morning he forgot to turn the fasset back, he was in such a hurry for fear the cook would catch him, so the hull barl of cider run away. Well, there's one consolashun. I herd papa say it cost a grate deal of money to eleckt a president. He said he'd been sent some and tole to place it where it would do the most good. I spose the calf and the cider must go in the eleckshun expenses. All I regret is they were not placed where they wood do the most good, cause me an Johnny were not allowed to eat and drink em. We expect to have a lot of fun next week. That freckle-face boy has walked past the house 3 times this morning. If Towser was not killed on the railrode I would set him on him.

CHAPTER XXIX.

HE MIXES IN POLITICS.

DEAR diry, did you know Lizzie fell into the cistern yesterday? Such a holring an screming all over the house an people running to get her out fore she was drownded, an Johnny's father's hired man coming over in a hurry with a ladder, you never see! He put the ladder down an fished her out and brung her up, an Bess she cot hold of her, an mamma was a screming to Betty an Cook to warm some blankets, cause she was so driping wet, an took the poor child away from Bess—and, after all, they found they nede knot have been in such a hurry—it was not Lizzie after all, but a false girl I made an thru in,— I got Lizzie to lie lo behind the woodshed wile I throwed it in an yelled "O, O, O, she'l be drownded—O poor Lib." So then they came and saw the dummy in the cistern, and began to make the offlust fuss. It was real unjust of papa to send me to my room without my supper, gust cause folks don't know a false girl when they see her. I never said she was in the cistern—I only said "Poor Lib, O! O!" So somebody left the lid up and the cat fell in, but I was mad an' did not say a word, so now to-day there is a grate surch for the cat—what has become of her?—I shall not truble to explane; they will know soon enuff when the water is scented with her remanes. I wish it was that sneck acrost the way who tumbled in and spoiled his new blue suto. Bess was expecting a few frends to spend the evening, and in the frite her angel-cake got burned up in the noven, so she had to come up to my room las night; it was Betty's night out, an she dasn't ask cook to see would I go down strete to the confekshunners an buy a pound of macroons and three kwarts of iskream, choclate an vanily mixed. You better beleve I said I would. It was much better going down strete to buy iskream than to stay in my room in a starving condishon, an hear the uther boys hoop as they run to the bonfire on the square. She gave me 2$ to pay for the refreshments, an I set out. " Now, Georgie, don't you be gone one bit over fifteen minits; the cream will melt like anything; you come rite back as kwick as your legs will carry you, that's a good boy ; don't stop by the way; we're all waiting for our cream; remember what perishable stuff iskream is; the evening is warm, will you hurry with all your mite, Georgie dear l" Sisters can be so offul swete when they want there little brothers to do anything for them. I ran all the weigh, an you bet I huried them up bout tying up the macroons an dishing that iskream in a pitcher so I could run home very kwick as Bess told me; but when I got home such a mess l that pitcher had about a pint of sloppy yellow stuff in it, an a little pup dog had et up all the cakes and even chued up the paper, but I didn't mind the paper so much. It is very strange how things will srink and srink up all like that iskream. I

spose I stood to near the bonfire made it srink. It was a beautiful blaze, sevral tar barels an a old kerosene blue hogshed. . Johnny an me an a lot of boys piled on the stuff as fast as we could. It lasted moren a nour. We stade to see it out, an such a hubbub! My only regret is that Bess-s company was disapo.nted in their refreshments. If I had known how it was going to be I mite have saved the 2$ an bought a lot of rockets. The yung gentlemun laffed and said, " O, if Georgie has had a good time at the bonfire never mind the iskream, Miss Hackett." But Bess most cride. So Mande Robinson said she would stay all night to our house—she is Besses most intimate frend since Sue marrid the doctor—an the weigh those girls sat up after the rest of the company went away I should think they would be so sleepy they would want to take a nap this afternoon. There is a wood fire in the grate, cause the evenings are chilly. They sat rite down on the rug. First they took oph their frizzes and let down their hair, an kiked oph their slippers an made theirselves comforable ; an then they begun to talk about the felloes. My! how their tungs did run on, an Bess said Mande should be first bridesmade, an then she sort of spoke lo, an said she, " Now, Mande, tell me true ; I know you are ded in love with him—you nedent be afrade to tell me—I'll never tell." An Mande she began to cry an sob an say, " O Bess, he dosent care a straw for me, an I love the—very grou—hound he treds on. Yes I do. I thin—hink ne's of—of—offul sweet. But don't you ever brethe a word to a living so—hole. No, indede ; it would kill me to have Char--har—lie Green dreme how I love him." It's a wunder I didn't pull the curtin down an betra my hiding plaice; but I kep very still, for I knu well nuff Bess wood pull my hair friteful if I let on, so I fell aslepe, an when I waked up they were gone, an then I slid up too.

This morning I was going round the long way to school to see what was up, and gaze on the ruins of the bonfire by daylite, when I saw a large groop of men about the town hall, on the steps an sidewalk talking about a parade an anuther torchlite processhun. Then I saw Charlie Green, with a lot of other yung men who belong to the Volunteers, els I wood not have thought about what the girls said. Its lucky I saw him, for now it is all rite. I said, "Hollo, Mr. Green ;" he said, "hollo Georgie, how's that iskreme this morning." Then I told him all—how those girls sat up comming their hair an tawking about him, and what Maude said, an showed him how she cride : the other fellows smiled, but Charlie got as mad as ever you saw, an said, "hush, George, you are a rude boy to tell things you overhurd." I said, "I thought you would like to know it, so's to go an see her an tell her not to cry any more," so I xpect he will call on her to nite.

It seems to me my father does not think or talk of anything but politix these days. He seems very much trubbled about the country. He says it is going to the dogs. I askd him what dogs. He said he meant it was going to pieces. I thought he meant an erthquake, like it says in my geografy, but when I asked him again he said, "O fug, I mean its going to fall thru." I wanted to know where it wood fall to—would it fall thru on to China an squash their pig tails, cos I heard a speker say the Chinese must go, an I thought papa was afraid America was going to drop rite down on China. He said I was a goose, not old enuff to understand the Chinese kwestion. But there semes to be plenty of fun in politix, such transparencies, such lanterns an flags an meetings an stump speeches an torchlite processhuns an bonfires it kepes a person busy. I do not have half the time to ackwire nolledge that I o to have; my techer says I must come to school regular or I will be a dunce. I must try an go more regular, because if I do not he is goine round to spoke to my father.

I did try to go to school regular yesterday, but I had a terribul sore throte an headache, so I could not eat my breakfast; mamma was fritened ; she thought it was diptheria. She gave me some medicine an said she would send for Doctor Moore if I did not get better; but I got pretty well about half past nine, so Betsy gave me 10 or 12 buckwhete cakes she had saved for me, an I sliped out the back gate to go to school. I thought I would go around by the depo to see the Volunteers board the train. They were to start for Blueville at half past 10 to goin the big celebrashun. Blueville is about 16 miles from here. There was going to be a grate time. Blueville is by the see. A clam bake, chowder, cider, a tent, Bob Ingersell, a crowd, a canon, fireworks, a brass band—of course when I got to the depo in the crowd an the train came in I couldn't help getting pushed rite up the steps into one of the cars. The crowd was so dense it utterly prevented my going to school. Before I knew it there I was, gammed in the isle, the train in moshun, not a cent in my pocket to pay my fare. Every time the conduckter went thru I went somewhere els, but he saw me after a while an asked me where was my ticket. Then I told him how I got crowded on, when I was just going to school, an some of the bon tons said, "O it's Georgie, we'll go his bale. I spose he wants to come along to burn up our ruther banner." So the conduckter said, "O it's Georgie Hackett, is it," an laffed an passed on, an in a little while we got there an I got off with the rest. We had a reglar 4 of July time. It was a little cool on the beech, but two enormus fires kept us about rite—one to make chowder, the other to roste the clams. There was about 1,000 more peopel besides our party. The band played, sevral gentlemen made speeches, an then we sung a fu songs and fired oph the cannon. I did not listen to the speeches, being very busy helping make a large iron kittle full of chowder an get a big pile of stones hot to roste the clams. I had no money, an I wanted to urn my dinner. I got a lot of scaweed to put round the clams to roste. There were barrels an barrels of them, an one barrel of big sea biskit to put in the chowder, with a lot of onyons, potatoes, pork, and salt and pepper. I cannot tell just how it hapened, but I got rolling the barrel of biskit an the pesky thing rolled rite slap into the wotter, an went out to see about 20 rods just as if it had set sale for Europe; then it swoshed back an a man waded in, but it bobbed up and down so it was a long time before he cot it—he ought to take a fish-hook, I think—but he got it, but they were soked through with se-wotter. The salt an' pepper were in there to, but forchunately it did not bust the pork. They had to make the chowder without any bisket or pepper. It put me iu mind of the story in my reader about the poor man's dinner. So the men thought I had better stay away till things were ready. Me an another boy took a stroll along the beech, an we come to a dead animal which looked very much like a jackass. It had washed ashore. I had read and herd a good eel in politix about boiled mule, so I thought this would do as well. So I told the other boy to look sharp when they had put the clams to roste, an we rapped it up in seeweed an waited till the men had gone to get a drink of cider an then we dragged it along with all our mite an plumped it on top the clams an put on more seeweed so they could have all the boiled mule they wanted

—only this was rosted—but I guess it was sick when it died, or had been kep too long, or something. When they took oph the seeweed to ete their clams—well, its perfectly offle to have more than 1000 hungry peopel mad at you, when you only wanted to give them a rare treat; but one man laffed and said he was glad it was defunked at last. I am afrade they had little to eat but cider, until they telgrafed to the city and had some cold vittles sent out. But the cclebrashun was golly; the band played, and about dark a large load of sandwitches an things arrived, and after we had eaten them we were going to have some magnifisent fireworks, only the car took fire in which they were stored an they all went oph together, witch was kwite too bad, for they did not last over 3 minnits all told, an you could not see the set pieces to any advantage. It was lucky the crowd was the other side the depo, or some one mite have got blowd up. A fellow took me by the sholder an asked me did I do it? He was going to give me to a policeman but one of our Volunteers come up an took me away—it was Charlie Green, that Mande is ded in love with; so he put me on a trane and pade my fare, an told me to be sure an get oph at the rite station. "I must not stay any later, our folks would be fritened about me, and it was dangerous for me to remane in the crowd; I had made myself so obnoxshus, some were in favor of linch law, some wanted to give me a notion bath for my helth, some proposed to make me ete a pcice of roste mule, I had better go home," Charlie said. So I went.

That is, I started all rite, but I was tired out, and fell aslepe in the car: and when I woke up it was midnite—deep dark midnite, an the conducktor said: "Sony, wake up we are almost in Philadelphia. Where are you going?"

CHAPTER XXX.

HE IS DISCOURAGED.

Not a friend in that grate city! Not a penny in my pockkit! Midnite on the deep! O, what a fraud are all our xpectashuns. I thought of all the little boys Id ever read of that got lost. I said to myself it was in this very city poor Charlie Ross was stole. I think I must have had the histericks, for I burst into teres an sobbed as if my heart wood brake. I am genraly ashamed to shed teres, they look so like I was a baby or a female, but I was dredful homesick an just a teeny weeny bit afrade something nite happen, my poor mamma would never see her darling child agane. A lady herd me sob an lened forward an said: "Poor little boy, is there anything the matter, have you got the stummikake? Here are some pepermint drops, take a fu." Then I tole her about the clam bake —how I got pushed on the cars on my way to school, and was put on the train to come home an fell aslepe, an went past our town like a streke an never knew it, an I had no money, an my mamma would be so fritened about me. She was very kind. She said I might go home with her an stay that night, an in the morning we would telgraf to my father to come an get me. I thanked her very politely, gus as I ought, an asked her had sheany little boys for me to play with till my father came. She said no, she was not married; but I did not ask her was she married—I only wanted to know had she any boys or girls for me to play with. I guess she was sick, for there was a carriage waiting when we arrived, an the coachman touched his hat very respectful, but he looked at me all over mity curious, as if I was the baby elfant or something like it. Then the lady says: "Mical, this poor child is strayed or stolen, we must take care of him to-night, an telgraf to his frends urly in the morning." "Iles a nice sweet lookin little chap," says Mical, "I ope he aint been an run away, like some of em does." "I will answer for him," said the lady. You bet her house was golly. O, lots handsomer than ours. She put me in a nice soft bed in a small room next to her oan, an left the door open so I would not feel strange. I fell aslepe in about 5 seckonds. My legs aked dredful, but I was 2 tired to mind that. When I waked up it was broad daylite; a neat servant girl, like Betty, said to me: "There is the bath-room. Missus says you had better take a bath. I have fixed the water in the tub gust rite—so get up, plose, an try it. Missus says plese dont medal with the fassets. In $\frac{1}{2}$ a nour brekfast will be reddy. When you are dressed come down stairs to the parlor." I had a splendid bath, only the tub got so full of hot water I had to gump out before long—I could not turn it back, the more I tride the worse it came, so by the time I had my close on, so I could go out an call the made, it run over the floor considerable. Forehunitly I found her goirg through the hall or the cealing would a been ruined—the girl said it had gust been freskode. I am afrade it made her some trubbel wiping up so much water.

I went down to the parlor; the lady was not there yet, so I looked out of the windo' There was a very pretty little girl playing on the side-walk. I opened the windo' an climed out an jumped down. She said "O my!" Then she said "Who are you, I did not know Miss Ward had a little boy stopping to her house." I told her how it happened. She was very sorry for me ; but she said if I was going to a celebrashun an get lost an everything, I ought to have put on my other suit, an not worn my school close. We played a spell an then she had to go to scool. I walked along with her a peace until sbe said I had better go back or I would get lost ; she pointed out how I was to go back, but I tried an tried and tried and could not find the house.

I was dredfully hungry. I think I rang about 200 door bells—all the rong ones. The knawings of hunger began to be terribul. Just then to my grate joy I saw her standing at a window. A man opened the door an let me in. She shook her head an said she was afrade I was incoridgeable

—I ought not to have gone out, specially out the window—I had made a scrach on her new paper an burglars mite have come in before it was shut again. I beged her to excuse me that once. I did not mene to get lost, but I wanted to speak to the little girl next door. She said she would that time—did I not want some brekfast ? She led me in the dining-room an sat down by the table while the waiter waited on me. I told her a good eel about myself. She wrote down my father's name an mine. I told her about Lil an the baby—how I was going to shoot it oph, an Bess an her bow—an my baloon experance last July, an mamma's an my trip to the Falls, an sevrul other things, and how I kept a diry. Sometimes she laffed and sometimes she held up her hands in horror. But that fool waiter, he dodged into the pantry and bust the buttons oph his vest gigling behind the door. I loved them snaps. So she said, when I had done cting, "George, I'm going round to the Continental now to telgraf your people to come on an get you. I leave you in Peter's my man's care ; I trust you will be a good boy until I get back. Here is a nice book to read ; you can remane here in the dining-room and read it until my return. I shall be home in less than a nour." She patted me on the head an give me the book an went out. Peter, he clored up the table, an then he went in the pantry to polish up the silver an wash the glasses. It was a plesant room. The sun shone in. There were two bird cages and the birds sang gaily. Miss Ward's speshal pet, a large sleke tortoys-shell cat lay on a quishon on the rug before a small fire in the grate. While I was reding I watched her wink in a knowing way at the canaries. The book was rather stupid ; I thought I would prefur to see what the cat would do. I just reched up an opened the door of one of the cages an then I read some more an watched the cat wink. In about a minnit a bird got out and flue around, having a good time. I think it is cruel to kepe birds shut up in cages so they cannot exercise. I read some more with I eye on the cat, an suddenly she gave a spring, when I just thought she was going to sleep. The canaries in the cage began to make a funny noise. Peter, he come in, but it was too late—that nasty grate big lazy tortoys-shell cat had killed that poor little incent bird ; its feathers were flying about. "Missus will give it to you now, young man," said Peter, " it was the finest singer of the lot. It will berake her heart, she was that fond of little Dick." Gust then I herd the hall door open. I turned red an pail. I tell you I wished I was at home. Miss Ward came in, all smiles. " I've had an anser, George," she said, " your father will be here on the 5 o'clock train," an then her eyes fell on the poor dead bird which Peter had placed on the table. "Who did it ?" she angrily asked. " Ime dredful, dredful sorry, Miss Ward, I am indede. I thought little Dick would like to fly about awhile. I cannot, cannot, tell a lie, The cat did it—nasty old thing."

She sat down and took the dead bird and cried over it till I felt like I wanted to sink through the floor. "You have broke my heart, George, I am sorry I brought you here with me last night. My poor Dick was worth all the notty boys in crissendum." Then I began to cry too, an told her how many times I wished I was dead or living on a dessert iland, so I would not get my kind frends into so many skrapes ; that I tried to be a very good boy, but was always in hot water till I was ashamed to be seen on the strete; then she said she wood try to forgive me this time; so I asked her why didn't she have a few boys herself an get used to them about the house. She said she was very glad she had none —she was going to leave her money to the hethen. I asked her was she an old made? An she laffed a little an said sum rude people called her so. I asked her didn't the fellows come to see her, but some ladies called gust then an she had to go in the parlor. " I wont be away long ; George, here's some paper and a pencil; would ruther you would draw on the paper than on my windows with your wet fingers. Try an pass the time as pashuntly as you can, we will have lunch when the ladies go away; dont touch the cages again, that's a good boy."

I drew the paper all over in a short time, an I looked at the cat an I notised how much her back was like a map of the world, the spots were the continents an' islands, the white places were the oshuns. Thinks I, they ought to be hamed. I heted the poker very hot, to draw the lines of longitude and latitude on her, and make it more nacheral, but I had only drawn about 2 lines, when she began to spit and yowl, an' Peter came out of the pantry to see what it was smelt so, an' that cat wouldn't hold still, but gumped right up on the sideborde an' nocked oph a blue china jug that had been in the family for sevral hundred years.

"Look a here, young chap," said Peter, offul sollum, "there was three things my missus set a heap of store by, her canary bird, her tortoys shell cat, an her blue china picher. The canary is dead, the cat is singed, the picher is broke all to flinders. If I was you, I'd put on my hat, an stay round outside till my father come for me." He said it so sollum an severe I began to tremble in my shoes. "Miss Ward is very benevolent," he went on, "but I'm afrade she'll send you to the stashun house. If she don't she ought to." "Let me stay in the kitchen," I said. "Humf! Cook will not have a child prowling around where she is." "Then I will go an stay in my bedroom," I ansered him, for I was too shamed an sorry to want to see the lady agane. I went up to my room an locked myself in. Miss Ward sent up for me to come and ete my lunchin. I hollered through the kehole I was homesick an did not want any. I guess she was tired of such a boy, for she let me alone. I cried for a little while, but when I thought it would soon be 6 o'clock I felt better. I opened the window and looked up an down to see if the little girl was

coming home from school. I saw several houses had flags out, so I thought I would rig up a flag. There was a red silk quilt on my bed, so I took it off and got one of the slats under the springs and pinned the quilt all along it and hung it out. Pritty soon lots of folks come up the steps an rung the bell. I herd one of the wimmen say, "I never thought Miss Ward would have a naucktion to her house. She must be going to go to Europ. I've always wanted a chance to set my foot in here, an now I've got it." Bout 20 or 30 peopel had gone in when Peter he comes to the door and looks up an down and everywhere till he sees my red flag, and then he shakes his fist and comes up to my door and orders me to hopen it; an he takes in my flag, an slams the window down, and says I'm "puffickly hawful." An Miss Ward she comes in, kind of crying and laffing both at once, and she looks at her watch an says, "thank goodness, Peter, its after 4 o'clock." An then she leads me down an makes me ete a enormus peace of cake an 2 creme-cakes an a saweer of charlot russ, and sets down beside me an kepes hold of 1 of my hands—like I was a kite she was afrade would sale away without leaf or lisense—au she says she wonders my mamma is alive; an at gust 20 minits past 5 the bell rings an I hear my papa's voice.

He thanks her 10,000 times, an says he hopes I have not given her much trubble, to witch she responds with a sikly smile, an he looks at me sharp from head to foot, and thanks her agane and agane. So then I throw my arms about her neck, an hug an kiss her an tell her how much I like her, an I wish she would come and visit me an mamma pritty soon; and we both shed a fu teres, an even Peter shakes hands, an I am on my way home.

Papa was very serius all the way home, an so was I. I xpect he was thinking what could he do with such a bad boy, while I was wundering how it hapened that a inocent child, who always tride to be an angle, should meet with so many axdents and have such a reputasbun. Ive got that ashamed of writing in the, my diry, so many mistakes an sorrors, I will bid the a long, long farewel, until I am thurrowly an xcelent child, like the good little boys you read of.

THE END,

BALLANTYNE PRESS; LONDON AND EDINBURGH.

Warne's 3s. 6d. "Hopeful Enterprise" Library.

With Illustrations, Coloured or Plain. In crown 8vo, cloth gilt.

Jack Stanley; or, The Young Adventurers. By EMILIA MARRYAT (Mrs. NORRIS).

White's Natural History of Selborne. Edited by G. CHRISTOPHER DAVIES.

Robinson Crusoe. By DEFOE. Unabridged Edition.

Swiss Family Robinson. New Edition. Unabridged.

The Schoolboy Baronet. By the Hon. Mrs. R. J GREENE.

The Young Lamberts. A Boy's Adventure in Australia. By AUGUSTA MARRYAT.

Heroism and Adventure. A Book for Boys. Edited by Mrs. VALENTINE.

Cavaliers and Roundheads. By JOHN G. EDGAR.

Among the Tartar Tents; or, The Lost Fathers. By ANNE BOWMAN.

Who Won at Last. By J. T. TROWBRIDGE.

Cris Fairlie's Boyhood: A Tale of an Old Town. By Mrs. EILOART.

God's Silver; or, Youthful Days. By the Hon. Mrs. R. J. GREENE.

Martin Noble; or, A London Boy's Life. By J. G. WATTS.

The Young Squire. By Mrs. EILOART.

Captain Jack; or, Old Fort Duquesne.

Edgeworth's Early Lessons.

Bunyan's Pilgrim's Progress. With Coloured Plates.

Sea Fights and Land Battles. By Mrs. VALENTINE.

Adrift in a Boat and Washed Ashore. By W H. G. KINGSTON.

Uncle Tom's Cabin. By HARRIET B. STOWE.

Bunyan's Pilgrim's Progress and Holy War. Large type Edition, with Illustrations.

Warne's "Holiday Keepsake" Library.

Small crown 8vo, with Illustrations, gilt, 3s. 6d.

The Woodleigh Stories. By the Rev. H. C. ADAMS.

The Falcon Family. By the Rev. H. C. ADAMS.

Gilbert's Shadow. By the Hon. Mrs. R. J. GREENE.

Mary Howitt's Tales.

New Edition. In crown 8vo, cloth, price 1s. each, Illustrated.

1. Sowing and Reaping.
2. Alice Franklin.
3. My Uncle the Clockmaker.
4. Strive and Thrive.
5. All is Not Gold that Glitters.
6. Love and Money.
7. Little Coin, Much Care.
8. Work and Wages.
9. Middleton and the Middletons.
10. Hope On, Hope Ever.
11. The Two Apprentices.
12. Friends and Foes.
13. My Own Story.

Warne's 1s. "Round the Globe" Library.

Large fcap. 8vo, cloth gilt, Coloured Frontispiece and Woodcuts.

Seven Kings of Rome, &c.
The Earth we Live on.
The Italian Boy.
Home Teachings in Science.
Our Ponds and Our Fields.
Brave Bobby, &c.
The Peasants of the Alps.
Frances Meadows, &c.
Uncle John's Adventures.
Casper.
Carl Krinken.
Frank Russell.
Tom Butler's Troubles.
Lizzy Johnson.
Mr. Rutherford's Children.
    Ditto.   Second Series.
The Children's Harp.
Charlie Clement.
The Home Queen.
Nellie Grey.
Clara Woodward.
Susan Gray.
Easy Rhymes & Simple Poems.
The Little Miner.
The Basket of Flowers.
The Babes in the Basket.
My Earnings.
Sam ; or, A Good Name.
Edith and Mary.

Willie's Birthday.
Willie's Rest.
Unica.
Mary Elton.
Pride and Principle.
Theodora's Childhood.
Mrs. Gordon's Household.
Little Nettie.
Fobert Dawson.
Dairyman's Daughter.
Jane Hudson.
Little Josey.
The Young Cottager.
Willie Herbert.
Old Gingerbread.
Tilly Trickett ; or, Try.
Alec Tomlin.
Hetty ; or, Fresh Watercresses.
The Children's Band.
Anna Ross.
The Romans and Danes.
Story of the Robins.
Dick, the Sailor Boy.
The Two Neighbours.
Father Phim.
Hapless Harry.
Pleasant Paths.
Little Threads.

In crown 8vo, price 2s. 6d , gilt.

PRINCE UBBELY BUBBLE'S NEW STORY BOOK

By J. TEMPLETON LUCAS. With numerous Illustrations.

Frederick Warne and Co., Publishers,

WARNE'S STAR SERIES.

ONE SHILLING VOLUMES.

Stiff picture wrappers; or, cloth gilt, 1s. 6d.

1 Daisy. ELIZABETH WETHERELL.
2 Daisy in the Field. E. WETHERELL.
3 Nettie's Mission. ALICE GRAY.
4 Stepping Heavenward. E. PRENTISS.
5 Willow Brook. ELIZABETH WETHERELL.
7 Dunallan. GRACE KENNEDY.
8 Father Clement. GRACE KENNEDY.
14 From Jest to Earnest. Rev. E. P. ROE.
15 Mary Elliot. CATHERINE D. BELL.
16 Sydney Stuart. CATHERINE D. BELL.
17 Picciola. X. B. SAINTINE.
18 Hope Campbell. CATHERINE D. BELL.
19 Horace and May. CATHERINE D. BELL.
20 Ella and Marian. CATHERINE D. BELL.
21 Kenneth and Hugh. CATH. D. BELL.
22 Rosa's Wish. CATHERINE D. BELL
23 Margaret Cecil. CATHERINE D. BELL.
24 The Grahams. CATHERINE D. BELL.
25 Home Sunshine. CATHERINE D. BELL.
26 What Katy did at School. S. COOLIDGE.
28 Wearyfoot Common. LEITCH RITCHIE.
29 Sydonie's Dowry. By Author of "Denise."
30 Aunt Jane's Hero. Mrs. E. PRENTISS.
31 Aunt Ailie. CATHERINE D. BELL.
32 What Katy Did. SUSAN COOLIDGE.
33 Grace Huntley. Mrs. S. C. HALL.
34 Merchant's Daughter. Mrs. S. C. HALL.
35 Daily Governess. Mrs. S. C. HALL.
38 Flower of the Family. Mrs. E. PRENTISS.

39 Madame Fontenoy. By the Author of "Sydonie's Dowry."
41 Toward Heaven. Mrs. E. PRENTISS.
42 Little Camp on Eagle Hill. ELIZABETH WETHERELL
45 Prince of the House of David. By the Rev. J. H. INGRAHAM.
46 The Pillar of Fire.
47 The Throne of David.
48 The Admiral's Will. M. M. BELL.
49 Sylvia and Janet. A. C. D.
51 That Lass o' Lowrie's. F. H. BURNETT.
53 Cloverly. MARY A. HIGHAM.
54 Alec Green. SILAS K. HOCKING.
55 Sweet Counsel. SARAH TYTLER.
56 The Milestones of Life. Rev. A. F. THOMPSON.
57 Little Women. LOUISA M. ALCOTT.
58 Little Wives. LOUISA M. ALCOTT.
59 Barriers Burned Away. Rev. E. P. ROE.
60 Opening a Chestnut Burr. Ditto.
61 Uncle Tom's Cabin. Mrs. STOWE.
63 Dorothy. A. NUTT.
67 Pine Needles. ELIZABETH WETHERELL.
68 Helen's Secret. DARLEY DALE.
69 Huguenot Family. CATHERINE D. BELL.
70 Only a Girl's Life. Mrs. MERCIER.
74 Bessie Harrington's Venture. J. A. MATTHEWS.
76 Without a Home. REV. E. P. ROE.
77 Moods. LOUISA M. ALCOTT.

EIGHTEENPENNY VOLUMES.

Stiff picture wrappers; or, cloth gilt, 2s.

9 Wide, Wide World. ELIZ. WETHERELL.
10 Queechy. ELIZ. WETHERELL.
11 Melbourne House. ELIZ. WETHERELL.
12 Drayton Hall. ALICE GRAY.
13 Say and Seal. ELIZABETH WETHERELL.
36 The Lamplighter. MISS CUMMINS.
37 Helen. MARIA EDGEWORTH.
43 Ellen Montgomery's Bookshelf.
44 Old Helmet. ELIZABETH WETHERELL.
50 Straight Paths & Crooked Ways. Mrs. H. B. PAULL.

52 Englefield Grange. Mrs. H. B. PAULL.
62 Little Women and Little Wives. LOUISA M. ALCOTT.
64 Leyton Auberry's Daughters. Mrs. H. B. PAULL.
65 Hedington Manor. By the Author of "Eildon Manor."
66 Without and Within. W. L. M. JAY.
75 Sceptres and Crowns, &c. ELIZABETH WETHERELL.

THE COMPANION LIBRARY.

TWO SHILLING VOLUMES.

In large fcap. 8vo, picture boards.

A COMPLETE COMPENDIUM of ENGLISH LITERATURE.

In crown 8vo, price 3s. 6d. each, cloth gilt.

Popular Readings, in Prose and Verse.
Edited by J. E. CARPENTER. FIVE DISTINCT VOLUMES, each Complete, paged throughout, with Index. A General Index to the entire Work is given with Vol. 5.

In fcap. 8vo, cloth, price 1s. each, 256 pp.

Carpenter's Readings, in Prose and Verse.
Twelve Distinct Volumes. Compiled and Edited by J. E. CARPENTER, Twelve Years Public Reader, Lecturer, and Entertainer at the Principal Literary Institutions in Great Britain.

A full Prospectus of the contents can be had on application.

In fcap. 8vo, price 1s. cloth.

Moseley's Readings. IN PROSE AND VERSE.
Embracing many of the Popular Readings of Mr. J. M. BELLEW, Mrs. DAUNCEY MASKELL, &c.

In fcap., Two distinct Volumes, price 1s. each, cloth.

Tom Hood's Comic Readings.
Embracing the Comic Readings of the last Hundred Years.

In fcap. 8vo, price 1s. cloth.

Choice Readings. Fifty-Two Stories of Brave Deeds.
Selected and Edited by the Rev. G. T. HOARE.

In 48mo, price 1s. 6d., cloth gilt;
or roan, pocket-book style, with elastic band, 2s. 6d.

The Bijou Gazetteer of the World.
Briefly describing, as regards Position, Area, and Population, every Country and State, their Subdivisions, Provinces, Counties, Principal Towns, Villages, Mountains, Rivers, Lakes, Capes, &c. By W. R. ROSSER. 30,000 References.

In 48mo, price 1s. 6d., cloth gilt;
or roan, pocket-book style, with elastic band, 2s. 6d.

Bijou Biography of the World.
A Reference Book of the Names, Dates, and Vocations of the Distinguished Men and Women of Every Age and Nation. By WILLIAM JOHN GORDON.